FERAL
DREAMS

Also by Stephen Alter

NON-FICTION

Wild Himalaya: A Natural History of the Greatest Mountain Range on Earth
Becoming a Mountain: Himalayan Journeys in Search of the Sacred and the Sublime
All the Way to Heaven: An American Boyhood in the Himalayas
Amritsar to Lahore: Crossing the Border Between India and Pakistan
Sacred Waters: A Pilgrimage to the Many Sources of the Ganga
Elephas Maximus: A Portrait of the Indian Elephant
Going For Take: The Making of Omkara and Other Encounters in Bollywood

FICTION

In the Jungles of the Night: A Novel About Jim Corbett
The Cloudfarers
The Secret Sanctuary
Neglected Lives
Silk and Steel
The Godchild
Renuka
Aripan and Other Stories
Aranyani
The Phantom Isles
Ghost Letters
The Rataban Betrayal
Guldaar

ALEPH BOOK COMPANY
An independent publishing firm
promoted by *Rupa Publications India*

First published in India in 2020
by Aleph Book Company
7/16 Ansari Road, Daryaganj
New Delhi 110 002

Copyright © Stephen Alter 2020
The author has asserted his moral rights.

All rights reserved.

This is a work of fiction. Names, characters, places, and
incidents are either the product of the author's imagination
or are used fictitiously and any resemblance to any
actual persons, living or dead, events or locales is entirely
coincidental.

No part of this publication may be reproduced, transmitted,
or stored in a retrieval system, in any form or by any means,
without permission in writing from Aleph Book Company.

ISBN: 978-93-89836-18-9

1 3 5 7 9 10 8 6 4 2

For sale in the Indian subcontinent only.

Printed at Replika Press Pvt. Ltd, India

This book is sold subject to the condition that it shall not,
by way of trade or otherwise, be lent, resold, hired out, or
otherwise circulated without the publisher's prior consent
in any form of binding or cover other than that in which it
is published.

FERAL DREAMS

MOWGLI AND HIS MOTHERS

A Fable

STEPHEN ALTER

ALEPH

for Shibani

Deep in the jungle vast and dim,
That knew not a white man's feet,
I smelt the odour of sun-warmed fur,
Musky, savage, and sweet.

Far it was from the huts of men
And the grass where Sambur feed;
I threw a stone at a Kadapu tree
That bled as a man might bleed.

Scent of fur and colour of blood:—
And the long dead instincts rose,
I followed the lure of my season's mate,
And flew, bare-fanged, at my foes.

★ ★ ★

Pale days: and a league of laws
Made by the whims of men.
Would I were back with my furry cubs
In the dusk of a jungle den.

—From 'Atavism' by Laurence Hope (Adela Florence Nicolson)

CONTENTS

Prologue / 1

I A New Jungle Book / 3

II The Foundling / 75

III Someplace Like Home / 149

IV Elephant Child / 197

Coming home—if you can call it that after fifty years—I didn't expect everything to look the same, yet little has changed. The canal road from Amrudpur to Shakkarganj has been paved, though it is badly potholed and just as rough as it ever was. Dusty villages along the way don't seem to have grown at all and the old mango trees that line the canal bank aren't any taller than I remember, though several have died. As the decrepit Ambassador taxi brought me home, I felt I was a boy of thirteen again, the age when I was driven away from here in the Miss Sahib's jeep with its canvas roof and the zigzag crack across one corner of the windscreen where I'd hit a cricket ball the year before. (She didn't know it was me who did it.)

I had no idea what would happen next. You grow up in a place and it becomes a part of you, so that when you leave, it feels as if you're cutting off your arm or a leg. Later on, there were times when I swore I would never return to India. I shut myself off from my past and tried to forget where I came from but that was impossible. Memories persist as does the language of childhood—my mother tongue. The last time I spoke Hindustani was in October when I visited Miss Cranston at the nursing home in Connecticut, where she had been living for almost ten years after dementia claimed her. She too had grown up here in Shakkarganj, a second-generation missionary whose parents started the orphanage back in 1923.

Reverend and Mrs Cranston's portraits used to hang in the dining hall of the Calvary Mission Children's Home. There was little resemblance between the Miss Sahib and her mother who had large, expressive eyes and a cascade of natural curls falling to her shoulders. The portraits were black-and-white, so it was hard to know if she was blonde or grey at the time. Reverend Cranston looked more like his daughter though he seemed to have been a sour-faced man with eyebrows that went in all directions like bristles on a well-chewed toothbrush and a thin unsmiling mouth. He and his wife are buried in the graveyard behind the ruins of the sugar mill, with matching headstones of discoloured marble. Their son, Ricky, Miss Cranston's elder brother, is buried between them. The chimneys of the old mill look like giant cenotaphs, rising above the other graves.

When I visited Miss Cranston two months ago, I found that she had reverted to Hindustani and none of the staff in the nursing home understood what she was saying. After I greeted her awkwardly with a 'Salaam, Miss Sahib', the way I always did as a boy, she got a look in her eyes that suggested there were shadowy memories there, though she did not recognize me. Miss Cranston spoke a dialect of Hindustani we all used in Shakkarganj. Most of what she said was disjointed and made little sense, with a few names thrown in, and mumbled lines about 'murghi nahin khaana hamney....' I'm not going to eat chicken and one phrase that startled me, 'Aa jao mere saath.' Come with me. For a moment, I thought she was speaking to me but then I realized she must have been talking to a childhood friend in her mind, one of the many orphans who lived on the compound long before I arrived there.

I almost wished I hadn't gone to see her like that, frail and feeble, slumped in a wheelchair on the patio outside her room. The nurses told me she hadn't had a visitor for several years and they were happy to let me meet her, though I didn't explain who I was. While I was there, the Miss Sahib dozed off a couple of times and I sat silently beside her as the afternoon sunlight streamed through rusty leaves on a maple overhead. It was a warm day—'Indian summer', as they call it here in New England. Her snoring was as soft as the purring of a cat but slower and uneven, not as persistent. I was about to leave when she woke up again and looked at me with a dazed expression. That was when I finally asked her, speaking again in Hindustani: 'Miss Sahib, yaad hai, main kaun hun?' Do you remember me?

She looked away, as if avoiding the question. I repeated it, then added, 'It's me, Mowgli.'

'Yes,' she said, quite loudly, and I knew I'd struck a nerve. 'Mowgli!'

'Are you sure?' I whispered.

She was shaking now, muttering to herself, and I couldn't tell if she had understood my question or not. By this time, the Miss Sahib had drifted off into some other subliminal layer of consciousness, the anxious tremor still there in her voice but saying something about watering the flowerpots...'gaindha' marigolds. And when I repeated the pet name by which she had always called me, there was no reaction.

I
A NEW JUNGLE BOOK
(Unfinished typescript by Elizabeth Cranston)

ONE

The boy climbed down out of the banyan tree and lowered himself to the ground by one of the aerial roots. It was late in the day and there was no breeze in the forest. Even the noisiest birds were silent and the only sound nearby was the humming of insects. Amidst still green shadows, a few beams of sunlight pierced the forest canopy, casting dappled patterns on the ground. Listening with his head cocked to one side, the boy could just make out the whisper of the river below, hidden beyond ragged thickets of bamboo. Drawing in a deep breath through his nostrils, he smelled the mouldering leaves and a sour earthy odour that he recognized as the passing scent of a sloth bear that had wandered by a short while ago. He was also aware of a lingering feline stench, where a tiger had marked his domain this morning, though it was so faint that the boy knew there was no longer any danger.

Peering up into the tree, he could see his companions, a troop of langur monkeys, sitting amidst the leaves with their long tails hanging down like furry vines. Fringed with silver-grey whiskers, their black faces were alert and wary. The monkeys would warn him if there was any reason to be alarmed, though every nerve in the boy's body was attuned to signals in the air around him.

Raising one hand he touched a spider's web and saw the tiny eight-legged hunter turn to face him, as his finger traced the delicate weave of filaments. One of the monkeys dropped a fig from above. Hitting the ground, it bounced near his foot. The boy picked up the green fruit and sniffed it, then took a bite. It had a bland flavour, still raw, but eatable. In addition to his five senses, the boy had a sixth sense too, an uneasy feeling at the back of his neck that warned him sometimes, as it did right now, like an ant crawling under his skin, a restless, prickling sensation that travelled from between his shoulder blades up to the base of his skull.

For a moment, the boy thought of retreating back into the safety of the tree, but his curiosity had been aroused by a strange object on the ground. It lay in the dead leaves, two or three strides away, a brightly coloured morsel unlike any fruit or flower he'd ever seen before.

The monkeys were watching him anxiously from above, waiting to find out what it was that had caught his eye. Edging forward, the boy reached down and touched the unfamiliar object with his fingers. It was no bigger than a pigeon's egg and rustled like a brittle cocoon as he picked it up. There was something hard inside and the boy sniffed it suspiciously. He could not recognize the smell, though it wasn't unpleasant. When he shook the object it made no sound. With both fingers, he began to remove the papery skin. The fragrance was stronger now but there was no fruit inside, only a hard, red seed the size of a pebble. Raising it to his mouth he licked it cautiously and was surprised by a sugary tartness on his tongue. After tasting it again and feeling a stickiness on his fingertips, he put the sweet in his mouth and sucked on it greedily.

Turning back towards the banyan tree, he felt a prickle again along his spine but the sour-sweet flavour in his mouth made him ignore the warning. Stepping around a fallen branch he flexed his arms, preparing to pull himself back up into the tree. But at that moment, he heard a hissing sound and saw a movement in the dust around his feet. Instinctively, the boy thought it was a snake and cried out. But before he could leap aside, a noose tightened around his ankle, yanking him into the air, so that he was hanging upside down. The sweet in his mouth popped out as he yelled and waved both arms, trying frantically to touch the ground with his outstretched fingers though the dry leaves and dusty earth were just out of reach.

The snare cut into his ankle painfully as the boy swung back and forth, desperately trying to break free. By now the langurs overhead had panicked and were all crying out in alarm. From their perch in the tree, they could see that the boy was suspended from a long rope, coiled around a supple branch. He shouted for help but only one of the langurs was brave enough to come to his rescue. Though he was the littlest of all, the young monkey swung down until he was level with the boy's face. Twisting his head around, the langur looked his friend in the eyes. The boy struggled to reach the tight rope around his leg, bending his body at the waist, while the langur tried unsuccessfully to untie the knot. The commotion in the tree above them only made things worse as the branches bounced up and down. Everything swayed and spun around so that the boy began to feel dizzy, until he heard a sound that made him stiffen with fear.

Human voices were calling out nearby and as the boy twirled helplessly in the air, he saw two figures blundering out of the jungle. The troop of langurs caught sight of them too and quickly sprang higher into the tree, except for the littlest monkey who stood his ground. He bared his teeth at the men as they approached but when one of them unslung a rifle from his shoulder, the langur backed away. He knew that the gun made a loud cracking sound and could kill an animal from far away. Reluctantly, the young langur crawled up onto a higher branch, watching to see what would happen next.

The two men were forest guards and the boy had seen them many times before, patrolling the park. He had always kept himself hidden when they were around. As the guard with the rifle came closer, he spoke in a loud, impatient voice that the boy couldn't understand. To him it was nothing more than a garbled set of sounds that made no sense.

As the second guard reached out to touch his arm, the boy lunged at him and bit the man's hand. With an angry cry, the guard took a step backwards. The littlest langur made a chattering sound and the other man threw a stone at him before taking a length of rope from his bag. Grabbing the boy by his long, matted hair, he turned him around and caught both of his wrists. Speaking to each other roughly, the guards tied the boy's arms together behind his back. Then the man with the rifle rested his weapon against the tree and unsheathed a knife.

Seeing the sharp, steel blade, the boy wasn't sure what this was, though he sensed it must be dangerous. Tugging at his arms, the guards pulled their captive down, bending the branch overhead. With his one free leg, the boy kicked at the men. Moments later, the rope was cut and he fell to the ground. Landing heavily on a rock, he felt a sharp pain shoot up his back and shoulder. Yet, within an instant, he shook off the guards and started to run. At the same time, the langurs began pelting the men with sticks and green figs.

If his arms hadn't been tied behind his back, the boy could have easily scrambled into a tree but instead he raced away into the jungle. Showered with twigs and fruit from above, the guards were distracted for a moment or two before they chased after him, shouting loudly.

Knowing there was a deep ravine nearby that led down to the river, the boy darted into the undergrowth. His one leg was numb from the snare and this slowed him down. Just as he reached the edge of the ravine, the noose, which was still around his ankle, got tangled in a thorn bush and he tripped. Close on his heels, the two guards tackled him as soon as he hit the ground. Though the boy fought back, they were stronger than him. Pinning their victim down, they tied his feet together. When he tried to bite them again, a rag was stuffed in his mouth.

The boy had no idea what the men were going to do and their harsh voices frightened him as he lay on the ground. A short while later, they picked him up, one of them holding his legs, the other lifting his shoulders and carrying him along a path through the forest. For a while, the boy could hear the langurs still coughing with alarm but soon they were out of earshot and the silent shadows of the forest closed in around them. Only the lone, little monkey followed overhead, slipping silently from branch to branch.

TWO

The guards carried the boy to a forest outpost nearby, where a shallow stream flowed out of the hills. In a broad clearing stood a small, single-storey building surrounded by a barbed wire fence. Parked in front was a jeep, which the boy recognized as one of the vehicles that drove along the dirt roads through the park. He had always been curious but afraid of these strange, wheeled creatures, which made a growling noise and gave off a sharp, smoky smell. Many times, the boy had hidden, crouched in a tree, watching the jeeps pass by and wondering where they were coming from and where they were headed. The tracks they left in the dust looked as if a pair of giant snakes had travelled along that route.

Often, there were other humans seated inside and whenever a wild animal or bird appeared, the vehicle would stop. Not long ago, the boy had been crossing the forest road, when a jeep suddenly came around the corner and almost ran him down. There was a loud squeal and then a hooting sound. Once the vehicle came to a halt, the boy had scampered away into a dense tangle of lantana on the other side of the road. Several times after that, he'd seen the guards tracking his footprints in the sand near the riverbank or along one of the muddy trails through the forest.

Now that they had finally captured him, he wondered whether they would tie him up like the animals he'd seen in the fields and villages at the edge of the forest. Though the boy recognized that he was similar to human beings in shape and size, he had never thought of himself as one of them. Having grown up in the forest, he felt more akin to the langurs and other animals in the park. Some of the wild creatures were still afraid of him though most of them understood that the boy posed no danger. He had learned to climb trees as easily as the monkeys but as he'd grown taller and heavier than the others in the troop, he had to be careful that the smaller branches didn't break under his weight.

Most of the time the boy was happy in the jungle, content to find whatever fruit or nuts he could eat, and careful to avoid any predators that might try to eat him. Occasionally, though, he felt a strange sadness, which he couldn't understand, like his sixth sense but deeper inside, between his ribs, an ache of loneliness that rose up into his throat and sometimes made him cry. When tears ran down his face, he became confused and wiped them away impatiently. The only other animals whose eyes watered like his were the elephants. He had often seen them shedding tears, as if they too shared the same unsettling sense of sadness.

While the men hauled the boy inside the forest outpost, the young langur watched from the trees at the edge of the clearing. Clambering down, he scampered across the open ground and crawled under the strands of barbed wire. Creeping towards the building, he was terrified that someone would see him but even more worried about his friend. Raising himself to the window, he peered inside and saw the shadowy shapes of men moving about while the boy lay trussed up on the floor. After a moment or two, one of the guards reached down and pulled the rag out of the boy's mouth. Then he placed a bowl of water near his head. The langur could see uncertainty and fear in his friend's eyes.

Rolling over onto his side, the captive raised his head and sniffed the water, which had a stagnant scent, though it was clear. He drank with thirsty gulps, as one of the men helped him by tipping the bowl next to his mouth. Some of the water splashed onto the floor but the boy was able to drink his fill. After this, the guard who had been carrying the rifle reached into his pocket and produced one of the same colourful sweets that had lured the boy out of the tree and into the snare. He removed the wrapper and held it under the boy's nose, offering it to him. Wrinkling his lips and baring his teeth, the boy made a snarling sound. He wasn't going to be tricked again. The guard laughed and put the sweet in his mouth. At the same time, the other man placed a white stick between his lips and lit it with a match. The end of the stick glowed as the guard blew smoke out of his nose. Its harsh, burning odour made the boy cough and sneeze.

Still watching from the window, the langur was relieved to see that his friend was alive, though there was nothing he could do on his own to set the boy free. By now the sun had disappeared behind the surrounding ridges and shadows flooded the clearing. Heading towards the trees, the young langur swung himself up into the branches again before setting off through the jungle.

A short while later, the forest guards went outside, leaving the boy on the floor. He tried to think of how he might escape but his hands and feet were tied so tightly they were growing numb. A few minutes later, the men came back inside and picked him up. They took him out to the jeep and put him into the back on a low bench seat. In the twilight, the boy could see the dark profiles of the trees and hills around him and smelled the evening scent of forest flowers that released their perfume after dark. This was the time of day when he knew he had to find shelter for the night. Helpless and afraid, the boy felt tears streaming down his face.

When the vehicle roared to life, his eyes grew wider and the tears flowed faster. He thought of his companions, the langurs, perched together in a tree and remembered the comforting warmth of their fur against his skin. The littlest langur had always been his closest friend. Like the boy, the young monkey was an orphan who had lost his mother soon after birth and had been raised by several of his aunts. Smaller than the others, he was the runt of the troop. As loyal as brothers, the littlest langur and the boy were devoted to each other. Often, the young monkey would hitch a ride on the boy's shoulder or perch on his back as he swam across the river. Now the boy felt he had been abandoned, utterly alone and bereft.

Two bright beams of light shown out of the front of the jeep, as they bumped along the rough, dirt road. The boy knew they were crossing a dry streambed and then climbing a low ridge, where the broad-leafed forest began. He had a map of the jungle in his head and a keen sense of direction. Growing up in the forest, he had explored every corner of the park and as the jeep passed through the tall trees, he could see its headlights flashing against their straight trunks. He also saw eyes glinting in the forest, a herd of chital deer and an owl that blinked several times before it flew away into the night.

The two guards spoke to each other as they drove along. Several times they looked back over their shoulders to see the boy huddled on the rear seat, staring at them with a look of defiance. His tears had dried and his mouth was clenched in an angry scowl. If his hands had been tied in front of him, he could have chewed through the rope. The boy tried to curl himself into a ball to reach the bindings on his ankles but the jostling of the jeep and the cramped space made it impossible.

Eventually, they started to descend a winding track and he knew exactly where they were, near a bridge above the confluence, where two rivers met. Here the road passed through a valley full of bamboo and creepers, a favourite place for the langurs because of the bean pods on the vines and all kinds of wild berries and nuts that grew along the riverbank. Just as they began to cross over the bridge, a large, hulking shape appeared in the headlights on the other side—an elephant! The boy cried out with excitement and relief as he recognized the matriarch of the herd with her flapping ears and swaying trunk. Behind her stood two other adults, each of them taller than the jeep, which came to a sudden halt. The guards looked nervously about while the elephants blocked the far side of the bridge.

As the vehicle began to move backwards the boy hoisted himself up to see if he might be able to jump out but then he heard one of the guards shout a warning. Immediately behind them loomed another huge shape and the boy knew it was the big bull elephant who usually kept to himself but sometimes joined the herd. In the glow of light from the jeep, his long ivory tusks shone like shafts of moonlight. Grabbing his rifle, the guard pointed it at the sky and pulled the trigger. Though the fire and smoke shot up harmlessly into the air, the boy's ears rang from the loud report. Instead of backing away at the sound, the tusker trumpeted angrily, then lowered his head and charged at the jeep. The boy could see the bull's rough hide and bulging forehead, almost close enough to touch.

The jolt of the elephant's weight colliding with the vehicle knocked the boy off his seat and onto the floor. The two men gestured frantically as they drove back across the bridge, where the matriarch and the rest of the herd were waiting. In the glare of light, the boy saw his friend, the langur, sitting atop the matriarch's back.

Trapped on the bridge, with elephants on either side, the two guards panicked. Leaping out of their vehicle they climbed onto a railing at the side. The boy couldn't see the river but he had often jumped from here into a deep pool of water that flowed beneath the bridge. As the matriarch stretched out her trunk to catch one of the guards, the two men scrambled over the railing and plunged into the darkness below. Moments later there was a loud splash.

The jeep had fallen silent and the boy could hear a soft shuffling sound as the elephants approached. Soon enough, he could feel their trunks nuzzling his hair and caressing his arms. The anxious, familiar gestures were comforting and he could hear the fluttering rumble of the matriarch's lungs, a sound that he had known from as long as he could remember.

THREE

The mother elephant's strong but gentle trunk wrapped itself around the boy's legs and lifted him out of the jeep. She held him up in front of her for a moment and he felt as if he were hanging from the snare once again before she placed him on the ground between her feet. With the tip of her trunk, she tried to loosen the knots on his hands but these were too tight. Just then, the young langur slid off the matriarch's back, down her flank and onto the ground. He made a chuckling sound to reassure the boy and then began chewing at the rope. The boy gave a grateful grunt and lay still until his hands were set free. His fingers tingled as feeling returned to his limbs, while the langur gnawed at the rope binding his ankles. By now most of the herd had gathered in a circle and they were sniffing and coddling the boy, until he found himself laughing with relief. Even the big bull came over to make sure he was okay and after puffing in his ear and nudging him with one tusk, he turned and headed back across the bridge. Passing the jeep, the huge tusker gave it a shove and flipped the vehicle over onto its side.

When the boy's legs were finally free, the matriarch picked him up again and put him on her shoulders, where he always sat, astride the nape of her neck, with his toes tucked behind her ears. The langur quickly climbed up behind him as they marched off into the jungle. For a moment, the boy wondered if the guards had drowned or whether they had been able to swim ashore. Relieved to be safely out of their reach, he wondered what the men had planned to do with him and where they had been taking him in the jeep. Of course, it didn't matter any more, now that he was safely on the mother elephant's back. Wagging his head from side to side, the boy began to mimic the men's voices. With a mischievous snicker, the langur joined in and they carried on speaking gibberish. After a bit, the boy pretended to steer the elephant, as if she were a jeep. Both he and the monkey made roaring sounds like the vehicle, until the matriarch got annoyed. Picking a leafy twig, she swatted them sternly to shut them up.

The herd walked through the forest for several hours until the moon came up and the matriarch decided they had gone far enough to stop for the night. By this time the boy had grown sleepy, lulled by the swaying motion, his shoulders slumped and eyes drooping. As she had done many times before, the mother elephant found a mossy, sheltered spot and plucked the boy and monkey off her back, laying them down between her feet. Both of them were tired and gladly curled up together. Occasionally there was the sound of a snapping branch as one of the elephants helped itself to a midnight snack but gradually they all fell silent. The younger ones lay down or leaned against their mothers but the adults remained standing in a protective circle. As he closed his eyes, the boy inhaled the grassy smell of the herd, soothed by the gurgling rumble from deep within the matriarch's chest. Moments later, both he and the langur were sound asleep, without a fear in the world.

In his dreams, the boy imagined himself running through the patterned shadows of forest leaves. He wasn't afraid, though he raced along as fast as he could, his feet skipping over bushes and rocks. As he came to a clearing in the jungle, where the ground sloped down steeply towards the river, the boy felt himself step out into the air, as if he were a bird taking flight. A sense of weightlessness and freedom made him laugh in his sleep, as he flew up higher than the trees, like the eagles and vultures that circled overhead. He could almost touch the clouds and was able to see beyond the edge of the park where fields and clusters of mud huts spread toward the horizon. The boy ran through the air, without getting tired, as if his feet were leaping from one treetop to the next, but just as he was about to reach the edge of the forest, he felt himself returning to earth, falling through layers of leaves. The dream ended before he hit the ground and he woke up with the sun in his eyes.

The elephants were still there but they had moved a short distance away, feeding on the fruit and leaves of wild jamun trees. As the boy rubbed the sleep from his eyes, he saw that the langur was also awake, sitting patiently by his side. As soon as he yawned, the monkey pounced on him and they wrestled for several minutes. Being larger and stronger, the boy fended off his friend before the two of them ran across and each grabbed an elephant's tail, pulling themselves aloft so they could reach the fruit too. After all his adventures the day before, the boy was hungry and he stuffed his mouth with the purple jamuns, as the juice trickled down his chin.

The animals and the boy did not speak to each other in the way that human beings do, but they communicated through sounds and gestures. Looking each other in the eye, they could express a range of emotions. The boy had no language of his own but he had learned how the animals voiced their thoughts, through calls of alarm as well as a touch of endearment or compassion. He could even understand most of the birds that called in the forest and knew what they meant by their songs and chattering. With the matriarch, who had watched over him since he was a small child, there was a special bond and she often told him stories as he leaned against her side and listened to the vibrations in her chest. Even with the others, the boy shared a forest tongue, as complex and intelligible as human conversation.

Picking ripe jamuns from the branches above his head and leaping from one elephant's back to the next, the boy could hear the youngsters in the herd, whispering among themselves.

Where do you think we're going today?

Not too far, I hope. The old lady made us walk all night.

It's the boy's fault. He keeps getting into trouble.

Hearing them talking about him, the boy dug his heel into the young elephant's back and then jumped aside as a trunk swung up to put him in his place.

It wasn't my fault! he answered.

Then whose fault was it? You know you're not supposed to go near the forest guards. How hard is it to just stay out of sight?

They tricked me!

If only you were a little bit smarter, came the retort, *but of course you're just a dumb runt of a human....*

I'm not human! the boy complained, spitting a jamun seed onto the ground.

Well, you're certainly not an elephant!

The monkey, who was hanging from a branch loaded with fruit, chimed in at this point. *He's a langur like me!*

The young elephants began to laugh together, a huffing, burbling sound.

So, where's his tail?

And what happened to his fur?

The boy began to get cross as he listened to their teasing.

Maybe he's a fish, one of the juveniles suggested, *a fish out of water.*

Or a bird without feathers!

Or a porcupine without any quills!

Enough! the matriarch warned them. *That's enough.*

But by now the boy had already jumped into the tree and climbed out of reach, where he sat sulking by himself until the herd moved on, browsing through the forest. Only the mother elephant stayed back, lifting her trunk into the branches, beckoning for the boy to come down.

Come on, she whispered. *There's no reason to be upset.*

The boy didn't answer, crossing his arms and pinching his face into an angry pout. His friend, the langur, had joined him and he did the same, imitating the boy's hurt expression.

Don't listen to them, said the mother elephant. *They don't mean any harm.*

I'm not a fish! the boy protested. *And I'm not a porcupine, either!*

Of course, you aren't, the elephant replied. *You're one of us.*

Then why can't I have a trunk and big ears like yours? he said.

Come down, she said. *It's not safe for you to be alone. The men will be looking for you.*

No! I'm not leaving! the boy insisted.

Me too! said the langur. *We're going to stay here and eat jamuns all day.*

The matriarch was silent for a few moments and the boy knew what this meant, though he remained where he was. Then he saw the mother elephant lean against the trunk of the tree and felt it begin to shake. She was swaying and rubbing her shoulder against the rough bark, until every branch swung back and forth, as if a sudden storm had sprung up with strong winds. The boy and the monkey tried to hold on but after a few moments the tree shook so hard the two of them tumbled off their perch and fell onto the matriarch's back, landing with a thump.

FOUR

After stuffing themselves with leaves and grass all morning, until the sun was directly overhead, the elephant herd arrived beneath a shady stand of teak trees, where they lay down for an afternoon nap. In case there might be danger lurking nearby, the matriarch took a final look around before sinking to her knees and rolling over onto her side. When a herd of elephants take a nap it can sound like an earthquake as the ground rumbles with their snoring. The boy didn't feel sleepy. He was about to follow the langur, who had set off to find the rest of his troop, but the mother elephant caught him by the leg and pulled him against her.

Stay here, she said. *I don't want you getting into any more trouble.*

But I don't want to nap, he protested.

Why not? the matriarch replied, drowsily. *There's nothing more delicious than falling asleep on a full stomach.*

She patted the boy's shoulder with her trunk as he rested his head on her belly and heard the noisy, gurgling sounds of the mother elephant's digestion. Her thick hide was tight as a drum and he listened to the vibrations that came from somewhere deep inside.

If you lie still, I'll tell you a story, she said.

Which one? he asked.

Any story you like…

Tell me about the time you first found me, the boy replied.

But you've heard it so many times already, she protested.

I want to hear it again.

For a few moments there was silence and the boy thought the matriarch might have fallen asleep but then he heard a patient voice, like an echo inside her cavernous chest.

A long time ago, during the rainy season, she began, *there was a storm that went on for days and days. It rained so hard that the trees cascaded like waterfalls and every path in the forest became a muddy stream. We didn't need to go down to the river to drink. All we had to do was lift our trunks and open our mouths and we could quench our thirst as water fell from the sky. It rained for five nights and five days until finally on the sixth day the clouds disappeared, and the sun came out. Every stream was flooded and many huge trees had toppled over because the soil around their roots had been loosened or washed away.*

I was worried that the young calves in our herd might drown as we wandered about in search of high ground. It seemed as if everywhere we went there was water and the earth was so soft we kept sinking up to our knees. The park was closed at that time of the year, because of the monsoon, and there were no human beings around, not even the guards. Every road had become a river. Deer and boar were stranded on patches of land, like islands in the flood, with nowhere to go. Most of the tigers and leopards had escaped to the hills. For three days, the water swirled about us until we finally came to a low ridge overlooking the grasslands, which had become a huge lake.

On the third day after the rain stopped, the water began to recede and we were finally able to march across the grasslands, though we made the youngsters hold onto our tails, so they wouldn't get separated from the herd. I was leading the way, as we came to a fork in the river, where the current was still swift and turbulent, though the water level had dropped. My plan had been to reach the opposite shore, where I knew there were a number of bel trees laden with fruit, which would have given us strength, but I dared not cross the river with the young ones.

Just as we were about to turn back, I heard a soft cry. It was a faint, whimpering sound like no other animal I'd known. With the rushing current of the river, I had to listen very carefully but I knew that something was hiding in a thicket of reeds along the riverbank. Sniffing the air, I couldn't make out any scent though the whimpering continued. Moving forward slowly, I parted the reeds with my trunk and there in the muddy shallows by the river was a small coracle made of bamboo and covered with buffalo hide. It had washed up in the middle of the reeds and was tilted to one side though it hadn't capsized. Lying in the centre of the coracle was a human child, wrapped in layers of cloth.

Was it me? the boy interrupted.

The elephant's trunk coiled around him as if the matriarch was remembering how she'd lifted him out of the coracle.

Yes, she whispered.

But how did I get into the coracle?

I don't know, she replied. *It's a miracle that you survived the flood. The swift current must have carried you down from somewhere high up in the hills above us, outside the park.*

How big was I?

About the size of a jackfruit, the matriarch answered.

He laughed, as he always did, when she said this.

It's a good thing one of the tigers didn't find you first, or else the coracle would have been empty. When I lifted you up in my trunk, you opened your eyes and stared at me, no longer whimpering. I still remember the look on your face, as if you recognized who I was.

The mother elephant glanced at him and then continued: *As you know, I used to live among human beings, for I was orphaned as a calf, just like you, and raised by a man named Arif Khan. He was a mahout for the Nawab who had a palace nearby. All this land, which is now the park, used to belong to the Nawab. Arif Khan was a kind and gentle man, not like some of the other mahouts who beat their elephants and mistreated them. He loved me very much and named me Mohua, after the fragrant flowers that grow in this forest...*

Mohua. Is that your name? the boy said. *You've never told me that before.*

Well, I don't really need a name any more, the matriarch said. *Since I returned to the wild. But that's another story...*

I want a name! the boy demanded with a frown.

I can give you one if you want, the elephant said.

Can't I choose my own?

If you like...

How about Jungli? he said. *Since I live in the jungle.*

The elephant made a snorting sound with her trunk that meant she didn't approve.

What's wrong with Jungli? the boy demanded.

I think we can come up with something better than that, the matriarch said.

Well, it's just as good as Mohua! he said. *Besides, who would ever think of naming an elephant after a flower?*

The mother elephant snorted again. *I was a beautiful little elephant when I was younger, with pink freckles on my face and ears.*

I want a name that makes me sound fierce and brave, the boy replied. *Like a tiger!*

We could call you Monkey! the elephant suggested, *because after I found you, I handed you over to one of the mother langurs. She put you to her breast and let you drink her milk. You were so hungry, they had to pass you around and you nursed from each of the mothers in the troop.*

But I'm not a monkey, am I? the boy said.

No, that's true, said the mother elephant closing her eyes with a sleepy sigh.

Wait, you haven't finished the story!

Yes, I have, the elephant mumbled, only half-awake. *We found you…we fed you…and then we all lived happily ever after.*

The boy made a disappointed face, as the matriarch began to snore, in chorus with all the others in the herd.

Jungli, he said to himself several times. *Jungli…Jungli?*

Then he crawled up onto the matriarch's shoulder and crouched by her ear as she dozed. Leaning forward, he whispered.

*Mohua…*and then a little louder, *Mohua.*

The elephant flapped her big ear, as if an annoying, buzzing fly was disturbing her nap.

Standing up, the boy raised both his arms as if reaching for the sky.

Monkey! Jungli! he shouted. *Mohua! Jungli!*

The mother elephant opened one eye as he jumped up and down, then with a drowsy mumble she said, *Mowgli…. That's what we'll call you.*

Mowgli! said the boy, with a satisfied smile.

FIVE

By early evening, the troop of langurs had congregated in a tall silk cotton tree near the elephant herd and Mowgli scrambled up to join his friends. The littlest langur greeted him with a leaping embrace and the boy had to quickly grab a branch to keep from falling to the ground. Without a tail, he didn't have the same sense of balance, though he had learned to move about in the trees with almost as much agility as the langurs.

Did you hear? The young monkeys chattered in chorus. *Those men that captured you...and tried to take you away, they didn't drown in the river.... Must have swum ashore.... This morning we saw them at the bridge, with some of the other guards...they were able to turn the jeep over and drag it away behind another vehicle, though it was bent out of shape.*

Mowgli nodded and laughed. *I think they'll stay away from elephants for a while.*

And you should stay away from humans, one of the older langurs scolded. *If you aren't careful, they'll dress you up in clothes and cut your hair and teach you how to speak like them.*

The boy stood up on the branch and picked one of the scarlet flowers from a cluster of blossoms hanging above. Instead of stuffing it in his mouth, as the monkeys were doing, he tucked it behind his ear with a cocky gesture that made the older langurs frown with disapproval. Sometimes the boy had the arrogance of a human being, showing off in front of the others.

Slapping his chest, he announced: *I've got a name.*

A name? the littlest langur asked. *What's that?*

It's something you call yourself and others can call you.

How did you get it?

The matriarch gave it to me, the boy replied. *She used to have a name herself, when she lived among humans.*

The monkeys looked puzzled, scratching their heads.

From now on, you can call me Mowgli! said the boy.

Mowgli? The langurs looked at each other. *Mowgli? What does that mean?*

It means Me! The boy cried, throwing his arms wide open.

But why do you need a name if we already know who you are? said one of the langurs. *It sounds like something humans would have, not us.*

Just then, one of the younger monkeys leapt onto Mowgli's shoulder and grabbed the flower from behind his ear before jumping into the safety of her mother's arms, nibbling on the blossom mischievously.

Mowgli bared his teeth and pretended to snarl, then shook his head and laughed.

I am Mowgli! he cried. *Everyone must call me by my name.*

Below the tree, the matriarch was listening. Raising her trunk she let out an impatient snort.

Mowgli! she said in a stern voice. *Just because you've got a name doesn't make you any better than anyone else.*

The older langurs nodded, picking the silk cotton flowers and eating them as it grew dark. Mowgli plucked a few buds and chewed on them, though he didn't like the flavour much. He preferred eating jamuns or other fruit. Now that he had a name, he felt different from the langurs. A short while later, his friend sidled over and whispered: *I want a name too.*

Let me think, said Mowgli. *I'll come up with the perfect name for you.... I know, we'll call you Chutku!*

His friend gave him a suspicious glance then shrugged, smiling as he repeated his new name: *Chutku.*

At the same moment they heard the alarm call of a barking deer from somewhere near the river. All the langurs pricked up their ears and looked around. The sharp cry of the deer was repeated several times. Then, after a few seconds, the alarm was picked up by a flock of babblers that started to chatter all at once. This was followed, soon afterwards, by the wail of a peacock that flew up into a tree nearby. By now the elephants had drifted away, out of sight. A chital deer took up the alarm with its high-pitched warning cry.

Something dangerous was moving through the jungle and coming in their direction. In the twilight, the monkeys waited to see what it might be—a leopard or a tiger. Mowgli and his friend crouched on the branch, not moving a whisker, as the chital kept calling. Suddenly, one of the langurs higher up in the tree gave a cough of alarm and a couple of male monkeys made a deep booming sound. Mowgli's eyes searched the shadows for any sign of the predator until he finally saw a movement in the grass. Though he was safe on the high branch, his whole body trembled with fear and his mouth was dry. The swaying grass began to part and he saw a blurred shape emerge in the half-light.

It was a man!

Unlike the guards, this human was barefoot and wore different clothes, though he carried a gun. A second man emerged from the grass, looking about him nervously and glancing up at the langurs, who had fallen silent now that they saw it wasn't a tiger. Following the other two was a third man, carrying a bundle over one shoulder. Mowgli couldn't see their faces but he sensed that the men were trying to move as stealthily as possible. Leaning against the trunk of the silk cotton tree, the boy hid himself as best he could.

The three figures stopped directly below him. Placing the bundle on the ground, they lit a match and Mowgli could see that each of them had sticks in their mouths. Moments later, a cloud of bitter smoke rose up into the tree and the boy sniffed at the burning odour, then sneezed. Instantly, the men looked up with surprise, recognizing the sound. The burning tips of their sticks were glowing ominously in the fading light. One of the langurs coughed to distract them and the men muttered among themselves in their own strange language.

Finally, they threw their smoking sticks on the ground and got ready to leave but before they could pick up the bundle there was a sudden thrashing of branches and four of the elephants burst out of the forest nearby. Mowgli could feel the thunder of their heavy feet all the way up in the tree. Instantly, the three men raced away from the spot, running for their lives in panic.

The elephants chased the men for a short distance and then turned back, snuffling with amusement and shaking their heads from side to side. When they passed the bottom of the tree, they stopped to sniff at the bundle and rolled it over with their trunks. The bag was tied up at one end and they weren't able to discover what was inside. Eventually, they got bored and sauntered off to rejoin the herd.

By now it was almost completely dark, though the sky was still a pale shade of grey. Mowgli could see the bundle lying amongst the buttressed roots of the silk cotton tree. Watching closely, he thought he saw it move.

Don't even think about it, one of the mother langurs warned him, knowing exactly what was going through the boy's mind.

Remember what happened last time.

Mowgli glanced around him and knew that he should stay where he was, but his curiosity made him drop down to the lowest branch, which was still high above the ground, twice as high as an elephant's back. Peering into the shadows below, he saw the bundle begin to twitch and squirm.

Those men caught something and it's trying to get out! he said.

Let it be, the mother langur replied. *We can see what it is in the morning.*

But what if the men come back?

It's not our problem, came the reply.

Mowgli listened to the huddled figures with their long furry tails and knew that he should stay where he was but then he remembered how he'd felt being tied up in the jeep. Maybe there was another creature trapped inside the bag who needed his help.

Wrapping his arms and legs around the smooth trunk of the silk cotton tree, the boy slid down to the ground, terrified but determined to find out what the bundle contained.

The burlap sack was tied at one end. As Mowgli gingerly touched the bag, he could feel something hard, curled up into a ball. He wondered if it was a turtle, though it seemed too large. Feeling the shape inside the bag, he thought it might be a fish because it had a long tail and wriggled at his touch. Nervously, Mowgli began to loosen the knot, looking over his shoulder into the shadows of the forest. If a tiger or leopard was nearby, he wouldn't be able to escape but as he listened there wasn't a sound, except for the soft *chuck chuck...chuck chuck* of a nightjar and the shrill song of a cricket somewhere in the leaves. Mosquitoes whined in his ear and he slapped at them. His sixth sense didn't send any signals of alarm. The rough cord that was wrapped around the sack took a lot of effort to untie and Mowgli finally used his teeth to pull one end of it free. Opening the bundle, he stepped backwards, eyes wide open with nervous expectation.

For a minute or more nothing happened and then he saw the sack begin to move. Very slowly a creature emerged. In the dim light, it was difficult to make out what it was, with a long snout and scales like a fish, though the animal dragged itself out of the bag with clawed feet. Mowgli had never seen anything like this before. It looked like a cross between a lizard and a cat but it wasn't either of those animals. As it glanced around and spotted Mowgli, the creature quickly curled up into a ball, its long tail shielding its head.

At the same time, one of the oldest langurs in the troop dropped down beside him and studied the strange species in front of them.

It's a pangolin, he said. *I saw one years ago but they're very rare. It's a kind of anteater. They spend most of their time underground. Those men are poachers, who capture and kill animals in the park.*

The elderly langur took a few steps forward and touched the pangolin, which curled up even tighter, though after a few minutes it lowered its tail and peered up at the monkey with a frightened expression.

Go on, get out of here, the langur murmured with an anxious gesture. *You're free! Go and hide!*

The pangolin made no sound but gradually stretched out to its full length. In the half-light, Mowgli couldn't tell which was the front end and which was the back.

Hurry, urged the old langur. *Get away from here as fast as you can. Find some place safe before those men come back.*

Glancing suspiciously at Mowgli, the anteater crept away slowly through the dead leaves, stopping for a moment to sniff at a termite castle before trundling away into the darkness.

SIX

The poachers returned the next day to retrieve the pangolin. When they found their empty sack, they looked confused and annoyed, casting about to try and find the animal's trail but by now the anteater had long since disappeared. Mowgli and Chutku watched from a tree nearby, hidden within its leafy branches. From the way the men reacted, Mowgli could tell that the pangolin must be a rare and valuable creature, though he couldn't understand why anyone would want to catch something that looked as strange as that.

Picking up the burlap sack, the three men finally headed down to the river. Moving silently from one tree to the other, Mowgli watched as the poachers began to wade across where the current fanned out into a shallow stretch of water that came up to their knees.

When the men were halfway across, there was the sound of an engine and a vehicle appeared at the edge of the forest. Four guards jumped out of the jeep and began to run towards the river, shouting. Immediately, the other three men hurried across, splashing onto the opposite shore. One of the poachers, who had a gun slung over his shoulder, turned and fired at the guards who dropped to the ground. At first, Mowgli thought one of them was hurt but they took cover behind a large boulder, as the three poachers raced into the trees. Mowgli guessed they were probably escaping towards the edge of the park, on the other side of a low ridge, where the fields began.

By this time the guards had run back to their jeep and had driven off in a hurry. Heading for the bridge upriver, they could circle around to the other side but Mowgli knew that by then the intruders would have easily escaped. Watching the encounter, he began to wonder what was taking place. Earlier, he had thought of the guards as bad men, who wanted to capture him, but now that he had seen them chasing the poachers, he wasn't so sure. The behaviour of humans was much too confusing for him to figure out.

Just then, he heard a sound from behind him and Chutku gestured for Mowgli to follow.

Come on, he cried. *We're going to eat mangoes today.*

Mowgli hesitated but the thought of mangoes was difficult to resist. He knew there were many orchards outside the park, where he and the langurs had feasted before. It was that time of the year again and his mouth began to water as he thought about the ripening fruit.

It took them a while to catch up with the rest of the monkeys. At several points, where the trees thinned out, Mowgli had to leap down and run along the ground. Chutku jumped onto his back when he did this, clutching the boy's hair. As they scrambled up into the trees again, Chutku let go and grabbed onto a branch. Though he was slow moving on the ground, because of his size, in the trees he was quicker than the boy. When they joined the rest of the troop, the older langurs looked at them with disapproval.

Reaching the last line of trees at the edge of the park, they could see a dirt track beneath them and a fence of barbed wire, beyond which lay a wheat field, recently harvested. On the other side of the field was an orchard. Even from this distance, Mowgli could see the green and yellow fruit hanging from the branches, waiting to be picked.

Sitting in the shade of the mango trees was a group of men with bamboo staves and lying beside them on the ground were a pair of ferocious-looking dogs. There was no way the langurs could approach the orchard without being seen. Mowgli's stomach growled and Chutku made a disappointed sound between a whimper and a sigh. The leader of the troop wrinkled his brow and studied the problem with a thoughtful expression. After a few moments of silence, he signalled to three of the strongest and fastest langurs.

Come with me, the leader said, pointing some distance away to the right. *There's a field of tomatoes over there. If we head in that direction, they'll chase us and once they're away from the orchard, the rest of you can go and eat your fill.*

The four big langurs scrambled down and began loping across open ground in the direction of the field of tomatoes. Almost immediately, one of the dogs spotted them and began to bark. The men got to their feet as the two dogs set off in pursuit. As soon as they saw where the langurs were headed, the men began waving their sticks and followed the dogs. For a few minutes the rest of the troop remained hidden. Then, as soon as the farmers were a good distance away from the mangoes, they all swarmed down from the trees. After crawling under the rusty strands of barbed wire, Mowgli let Chutku jump on his back and set off running across the field. Nobody made a sound and they reached the trees before the farmers had any idea of what was happening. As quickly as possible, they scampered into the branches and began picking the fruit. Mowgli took one mango in each hand and bit into the leathery green skin. Then squeezing the fruit with his fingers, he sucked the pulpy juice from one and then the other. Chutku peeled his mango with his teeth and took big bites of the yellow flesh, the sticky juice dribbling onto his fur.

Mowgli kept a sharp eye on the farmers and their dogs, who were chasing the other langurs. The leader of the troop had vaulted over the fence of thorns surrounding the tomato field but as soon as the dogs arrived, the langurs leapt across to the other side and headed back toward the forest.

When the farmers stopped and turned around, they saw the rest of the monkeys feasting in the orchard and they cried out in alarm. Soon enough, the men and dogs were racing back to protect the crop and the langurs quickly fled towards the forest, carrying whatever fruit they could. Mowgli had picked two mangoes to give to the leader of the troop and he gestured for Chutku to hurry up. As soon as they landed on the ground, the young langur jumped onto his back and they sprinted for cover.

Behind them, they could hear the dogs baying and the farmers cursing but by now most of the langurs had already made it back to the safety of the trees. Mowgli could see the barbed wire fence ahead but as he got ready to dive under it, his foot tripped on the stubble of wheat and he fell and rolled over. Chutku tumbled off and the two of them landed flat on their faces. The dogs were close behind them and Mowgli saw Chutku trying to retrieve a mango he'd dropped.

Leave it! he cried.

When the little langur looked up, one of the dogs was almost upon him. Mowgli immediately picked up a clod of earth and threw it at the dog, who yelped and retreated, then bared his teeth. Chutku scrambled under the fence as quickly as he could and made his way safely to the nearest tree.

Meanwhile the two dogs had cornered Mowgli with his back to the fence, snarling and gnashing their teeth. The farmers had seen him as well and they began to call out to the boy in angry, threatening voices. Mowgli looked the dogs in the eyes, wishing he could say something so they'd leave him alone. But like the men, these animals didn't understand the language of the wild.

In desperation, he threw another clod of dirt at the dogs. When they flinched and retreated, he dove beneath the barbed wire and ran for his life. The sharp metal points cut through his skin and he felt a tearing pain in his back. As he lunged for the trunk of the nearest sal tree and pulled himself up, he knew that neither the dogs nor the men could catch him now. The troop of langurs welcomed him into their midst as they hurried off into the jungle.

Later, as he sat in the crook of a large flame of the forest tree, Mowgli tried to see the wounds on his back but he wasn't able to turn his head far enough around. The blood had stopped flowing but the pain was still there and he knew it would be a while before it healed. Though he could still taste the sweetness of the mangoes, he wasn't sure he would ever leave the park again.

SEVEN

The day after the raid on the mango orchard, Mowgli set off on his own through the forest at dawn, following a trail he'd taken before. The wounds on his back were painful and he hadn't been able to sleep during the night. Though the langurs had tried to comfort him, he was restless and felt an instinctual urge to be alone. Moving as silently as a shadow through the jungle, he made his way into the hills towards the river and away from the rising sun.

By the time the dew on the leaves and grass had evaporated, he came to a narrow ravine between two slabs of rock, the opening just wide enough for him to squeeze through and clamber up a series of mossy ledges. Until now, he had seen no other animals but as he ascended into a shaded glen, a couple of deer slipped past him and he saw a wild boar rooting up the ground. A number of birds filled the trees including a pair of hornbills feeding on wild figs, tiny sunbirds sipping nectar and a flock of green pigeons camouflaged amidst the leaves. The secluded glen was a place where animals came when they were sick or injured. Most of the plants and shrubs that grew here cured diseases and helped soothe pain. Mowgli had been brought to the glen twice before when he'd had a fever. One of the elderly langurs had showed him which herbs and berries to eat. There were mushrooms too and trees whose bark and resin had medicinal properties.

As Mowgli approached, the boar glanced up, his snout and tushes caked with dirt.

Recognizing some of the herbs he'd eaten before, the boy plucked a sprig of leaves and put it in his mouth. Despite the bitter taste, he chewed and swallowed the herb. Snorting at him with an encouraging shake of its head, the boar uprooted a tuber that he nudged in Mowgli's direction. Picking it up, the boy brushed off the dirt and sniffed the twisted root, which was about the size of his thumb. The sharp smell made his nostrils burn but when he tasted the tuber it had a mild flavour like the wild yams he loved to eat.

The healing glen had a peaceful atmosphere and the cooing of green pigeons made the boy feel less anxious about his injuries. A few moments later, he saw a sleek shadow detach itself from a branch nearby and spring to the ground. Realizing it was a leopard, Mowgli took a step backwards though he knew that this was a protected place where predators and prey ignored each other. The boar seemed unafraid of the leopard and none of the birds cried out in alarm.

Rising up on its hind legs, the leopard unsheathed its claws and began scratching the trunk of a tree, raking the smooth bark in the same way the barbed wire had cut into Mowgli's back. After a few minutes, the big cat moved aside and turned to look at the boy. Though his yellow eyes had a menacing intensity, Mowgli could tell that the leopard meant him no harm. In fact, it seemed to be calling him closer with a low purring sound. By now, Mowgli could see dark streams of sap oozing out of the tree trunk. As he approached, the leopard withdrew, though he kept his eyes fixed on the boy. The resinous fluid that bled through the bark had a sweet fragrance and the boy gently leaned his back against the tree. At first the sap stung his wounds, but he knew that the leopard had guided him to treat the lacerations on his back. Soon enough, the sting was gone and he felt a numbness spread from his shoulders to the base of his spine.

After the boy stepped away from the tree, he saw that the leopard had vanished. Two pigeons fluttered down and perched on a nearby bush, which was budding with small yellow flowers. Making a soft, burbling sound they seemed to encourage the boy to pick the blossoms, which he cautiously put in his mouth. The flowers had a peppery flavour but a sweet aftertaste.

By now the boy was feeling drowsy after his sleepless night. The pain in his shoulders and back had diminished and there was only a dull ache beneath the layer of sap that coated his wounds. At the far end of the clearing, Mowgli spotted a cleft in the side of the hill, fringed with ferns. He knew it was the Medicine Cave, a secret retreat where wounded animals came to recover and regain their strength. For a brief moment, the boy was afraid of what might be lurking inside–bats and snakes, scorpions and toads–but he remembered how the elderly langur, who had brought him here first, reassured him that the cave was the safest place in the forest where nothing would harm him and he could forget all his fears.

Pushing aside the ferns, Mowgli entered the darkness and felt a cool, moist breeze blowing out of the cave. He inched forward, one hand brushing against the rocks overhead, as his bare feet left impressions in the powdery dust on the floor. No longer afraid, the boy moved forward until the light from the mouth of the cave was extinguished and the darkness was complete. All around him, he could smell animal scents and hear the muffled breathing of other creatures that had sought the sheltering succour of the Medicine Cave.

As he felt a gentle lethargy overwhelm his body, the boy lay down on the floor of the cave with his back to the rough rock wall. Yet, the hard stones felt as soft as a pallet of straw and the darkness closed in around him with a comforting intimacy, as if an invisible caregiver had picked the boy up in her arms. The second he closed his eyes, Mowgli passed immediately into a deep sleep that was free of dreams. The shadowy interior of the Medicine Cave held him in its calm embrace as the herbs erased his pain and the sap from the tree healed his wounds.

Much later, when he finally awoke, Mowgli had no idea where he was though he felt no fear and understood that he was protected by the darkness. Rested and feeling strong, he rose slowly to his feet and recalled the scratches on his back, though there was no pain or swelling, only a faint itch of irritation. Feeling his way through the hollow chamber in the rocks, he retraced his steps until the slit of green light appeared ahead of him, where ferns enclosed the mouth of the cave.

Emerging into daylight, it took several minutes before his eyes adjusted to the brightness. He had no idea how long he had been in the cave; it could have been several days or less than an hour. The boar was gone and the leopard too. Instead, a herd of black buck was grazing on the grass. The antelopes ignored him as he walked by but in the tree above, he saw a striped squirrel watching him as well as an owl peering out from a hole in the trunk.

Plucking a handful of herbs, the boy nibbled on them as he found his way to the lip of the ravine, where he scrambled down the rocks and back out into the main forest below. The urge to be alone was gone and he set out to find his companions, the langurs, though he had no idea where they might be. The trail that had brought him here continued along the base of the foothills and across a patch of degraded scrubland, which had burned in a fire several years ago. The blackened trunks of dead trees protruded above the underbrush, stark reminders of the destructive wildfire. The boy could remember the billowing clouds of smoke and dancing flames that had left the ground scorched and buried in ash.

Beyond this scarred patch of jungle, lay thickets of bamboo that stood on a high bank above the river. The heat of the sun on his back made the scabs from his wounds prickle and itch. By the time he parted the supple stems of bamboo and looked down at the water, Mowgli was ready for a swim.

To his delight, he saw that the elephant herd had got there before him and they were already in the water. Some were standing near the shore, spraying themselves, while others lay in the middle of the current, letting the water flow around them as if they were huge rocks dividing the stream. Mowgli gave a whoop of excitement and raced down the steep slope. The hot sand burned his bare feet as he dashed headlong into the river, diving eagerly beneath the surface. The matriarch was swimming a short distance downstream where the river narrowed into a deep pool and the current swirled against a cliff, circling back upon itself.

The mother elephant reached across with her trunk and lifted Mowgli out of the water, his long hair streaming and his legs kicking as if to escape, though he laughed with pleasure. After plunging into the water again, he surfaced near the elephant and told her how he'd injured himself on the barbed wire. Then he explained that he'd gone to the Medicine Cave alone, seeking solace and healing.

With her trunk, the matriarch inspected his back, as she questioned him, concerned and comforting. The water had washed away the tree sap and his skin had closed over the wounds. Diving beneath the elephant, Mowgli swam between her legs, which stood on the pebbled bottom. Ahead of him, he saw a school of fish escaping upstream with two lithe shapes in pursuit. Surfacing and taking a deep breath, Mowgli came face to face with a pair of otters that blinked at him with surprise. Their smooth wet fur made it look as if they were part of the water and their whiskers twitched in irritation for the boy had scared off the fish they had hoped to catch. With an agile twist of their bodies, the otters dove beneath the surface again, splaying their webbed paws. The boy tried to follow, dipping under for a moment, before he felt the mother elephant's trunk catch him by one ankle and hold him fast. As he floundered back up to the surface, sputtering and coughing, Mowgli gave the matriarch an irritated scowl. Drawing Mowgli against her broad flank, the elephant pointed with her trunk.

On a narrow shelf at the foot of the cliff, overlooking the pool, lay a still grey shape, the same colour as the stones. It was a mugger crocodile and its cold-blooded gaze was fixed on the boy.

EIGHT

When the elephants had finished bathing, they headed up the riverbank with Mowgli riding on the matriarch's back. He felt calm and refreshed, at peace with himself and the world. The herd took its time entering the forest, feasting on bamboo and other grasses, as Mowgli listened to birdcalls that rang out on all sides–the shrill cry of a serpent eagle, circling overhead, the piping call of a pair of lapwings and the cawing of jungle crows, as well as the twittering of leaf warblers. Then amidst the chorus of birdsong he heard a muted whistle that immediately caught his ear. It was repeated several times and Mowgli listened attentively, trying to locate the sound. He knew it wasn't a bird.

There were several different whistles, each of a varying pitch. The boy knew what animal made this sound and he could imitate the call by blowing through his pursed lips. The elephants also reacted to the whistles, cautiously raising their trunks to catch a scent, aware that a hunt was underway. Mowgli heard the alarm cry of a chital. As the herd moved forward between the trees, his eyes scanned the jungle ahead of him for movement. Eventually, he spotted a flash of reddish fur racing through a lantana thicket. The whistles had now become more insistent, each piercing note punctuating the silence of the forest.

As the mother elephant pushed her way through a barricade of thorny shrubs, they came to an open patch of grass surrounding a seasonal waterhole. The ground was pockmarked with the hoof prints of deer and boar but the murky puddle in the centre had almost dried up.

Suddenly, a small, agile creature with dusty red fur burst out of the grass to their right and gave a soft whistle. Mowgli knew that the dhole, or wild dog, was one of the most dangerous predators in the jungle despite its plaintive, fluting cry. Within minutes, the rest of the pack appeared on all sides of the waterhole. The elephants stopped in their tracks, though the wild dogs showed no interest in the herd. With their ears perked and tongues hanging out, all the dhole were staring in the same direction. Moments later, a chital doe and her fawn raced out of the trees, their tails raised in alarm. A pair of dhole were chasing after them and drove them towards the centre of the waterhole. Both the mother deer and her fawn looked terrified as their hooves sank into the mud, slowing them down. Within a few seconds the pack of wild dogs had encircled them and began closing in. The predators were silent now, no longer whistling, sharp eyes fixed on their prey.

Mowgli had seen wild dogs only twice before. The dhole were much smaller than the farmer's dogs that had chased him away from the mango orchard, but when a pack of them hunted together they could kill animals as large as a sambar, running it down and biting its legs until the deer collapsed. Most of the wild animals in the forest were as frightened of these whistling hunters as they were of tigers and leopards.

The fawn made a terrified, bleating sound as it struggled in the deep mud, while the chital doe kicked one of the dogs that nipped at her hoof, frantically trying to keep it at bay.

Without thinking, Mowgli slid off the matriarch's back, grabbing her ear as he dropped to the ground. She tried to stop him with her trunk but the boy was too quick, running forward and letting out his fiercest roar, though it hardly sounded threatening, more like the yawn of a bear.

Three of the dogs turned to look at him, startled by this unexpected intruder who had interrupted their pursuit of a meal. The rest of the pack were still intent on bringing down the deer but as Mowgli waved his arms and bared his teeth in a snarl, more of the dhole caught sight of him. When the boy darted around the muddy waterhole, the leader of the pack let out a whistle. Each of the other dogs replied with their hunting calls as they turned in his direction. Sensing that this was their only chance to escape, the chital and her fawn scrambled out of the mud and raced away into the trees. A few of the dogs began to chase them but it was too late and the pack quickly regrouped, focusing on Mowgli with eager eyes.

Until now the elephants had watched the dogs without any reaction, curious but content to keep their distance. However, seeing that the boy was alone and surrounded by more than twenty of the whistling hunters, the matriarch lifted her trunk and trumpeted loudly. The dhole ignored her. With the cunning and teamwork of the pack, they closed in on Mowgli and cut him off from the herd. Realizing that he could not reach the matriarch to climb on her back, the boy tried to race across to the nearest tree but found his way blocked by a pair of dhole that had circled around from the other side.

Picking up a stick, Mowgli waved it at the wild dogs but they weren't afraid. The rest of the pack moved in closer. Even when he hurled a stone in their direction, the hunters drew the circle tighter, their bushy tails wagging and their ears twitching in anticipation. Unlike the farm dogs who had barked and barked, the dhole remained silent now, not even a whistle. Though he had been alarmed and upset to see the fawn and its mother surrounded by the dogs, Mowgli realized that he was in the same position now and there was no way he could escape. Baring his teeth, he tried to be brave but he knew he was outnumbered and trapped. As he started to run, Mowgli's feet slipped in the mud and he fell to his knees.

Just as the dogs' sharp teeth were about to find their mark, the matriarch decided she'd waited long enough. With another trumpet of rage, she charged the pack, followed by the rest of the herd. The wild dogs knew better than to hold their ground against these thundering giants who could crush them underfoot. Within a few seconds they scattered, racing away into the bushes, emitting a few frustrated whistles as they disappeared.

The boy's legs and arms were covered in mud but he was unhurt. Mowgli looked up at the mother elephant with a defiant expression.

You didn't need to help me, he said. *I could have chased them off by myself.*

Is that so? the matriarch replied. *I hope you've learned your lesson.*

What lesson? Mowgli mumbled as he got to his feet.

Think before you blunder into a situation where you can't defend yourself, came the reply. *It's all very well to feel sorry for another animal but that doesn't mean you have to put yourself in danger.*

The dogs would have killed the deer, he answered.

Yes, that's how they survive, the mother elephant replied. *It may seem cruel but it's the way of the wild.*

How could you just let them attack a defenceless little fawn? the boy insisted as he stomped out of the mud. *Don't you feel sorry for the deer?*

Of course, we do, one of the other elephants replied. *But if the dogs don't catch their prey, they'll starve. They won't have any meat to feed their young.*

Besides, we can't spend all our time defending other species, the matriarch added. *We wouldn't be able to feed ourselves.*

But it's not fair! the boy cried. *It's wrong to let another animal be killed!*

The elephants looked at each other with sombre expressions and shook their heads in unison.

It's neither wrong nor right, Mowgli, the mother elephant argued. *That's just the way it is in the jungle. An insect gets eaten by a bird. A bird gets eaten by a snake. A snake gets eaten by a mongoose. A mongoose gets eaten by a jackal. And so on and so forth, right up the food chain...*

But elephants don't kill animals and eat them! the boy cried out in frustration.

That's true, the matriarch replied. *We do a lot of damage in other ways, though. We knock down trees where birds build their nests. Without knowing it, we crush insects and lizards under our feet. Sometimes, we even attack leopards and tigers in self-defence. But that's what all animals do in the wild. It's part of the natural cycle of life. In fact, the only species that harms other creatures for no reason at all are human beings!*

The boy faced the herd with a puzzled expression and frowned.

Why are you staring at me? the boy protested. *I'm not a human!*

Yes, I'm afraid you are, whether you like it or not, the matriarch replied. *That's the reason you tried to protect the chital.*

Now the boy looked even more confused.

What do you mean? Mowgli said, folding his arms. *How can humans kill animals and protect them at the same time?*

It's one of the contradictions of your species, the wise mother elephant replied. *Remember, I lived amongst men for most of my life and I was able to observe how they behaved. Sometimes they are cruel and heartless. Other times, they are compassionate and kind. Your people can't ever seem to make up their minds.*

Hearing this, the boy fell silent, knowing that sometimes he himself had felt those same conflicting emotions, like a wind that blew in both directions tossing the trees back and forth.

NINE

Scrambling up the mother elephant's trunk and onto his seat astride her neck, Mowgli thought about what it meant to be human. Looking at his hands, he realized that his hairless fingers and thumbs were unlike those of any other animal, even the monkeys, and he knew that the footprints he left in the dust were exactly like those of a man. Sometimes, when he was sitting amongst the langurs, he watched the way they communicated with each other and noticed how every monkey recognized his or her place in the troop, from the youngest to the oldest, the weakest to the strongest. He wondered what it was that made them live together, rather than wandering off by themselves. His mind was so full of questions that Mowgli often got confused by all the different thoughts in his head. The elephants were the only animals that seemed to share his emotions but even they weren't easily upset or disturbed while Mowgli often felt agitated or alarmed and behaved impulsively, just as he'd done with the wild dogs and the deer.

There were days when he wished he could be as big as an elephant so that he could throw his weight around or as nimble as a monkey and climb to the very top of a tree. He wanted claws like a leopard and teeth like a tiger, and a bear's sense of smell. If only he could run as fast as an antelope or fly through the air like a bird. But instead, his body seemed awkward and thin, unsuited to life in the jungle.

For several hours, the herd of elephants roamed through the forest, browsing on foliage and uprooting tufts of grass. They seemed to be wandering aimlessly about, though all of them were feeding constantly. Mowgli couldn't imagine eating all day. Though he often felt hungry, a wild fruit or a handful of nuts satisfied his appetite for several hours.

Eventually, they came to a green pool of water, deep in the heart of the forest. Mowgli realized that the matriarch had been leading them here all along, though it had seemed as if they were travelling in no particular direction. He knew this place well for he had been here many times before and often swam in the pool, which was surrounded by reeds. As the mother elephant waded into the shallows to drink, the boy slid down her trunk and splashed into the pool. The mud from his morning's encounter with the dogs had dried on his skin but as he swam through the water, he felt it slough off and he dove under, imagining himself as an otter. Opening his eyes in the murky green depths of the pool he saw nothing at first, then spotted the long stems of water lilies rising from the bottom. When he surfaced near one of the lily pads, he caught sight of a small frog sitting on a floating leaf. A bright green colour, it was no bigger than the boy's nose. They looked at each other for a moment but when Mowgli put out his hand to catch the frog, it leapt into the water and disappeared. Closer to shore, a pink water lily was blooming and the boy swam over and picked the flower. Holding it in one hand, he waded out of the pool and gave the water lily to the matriarch, who took it gently in her trunk and inspected the delicate pink petals. Mowgli thought it was the most beautiful thing he had ever seen but the elephant had other ideas. With a grateful blink of one eye, she popped the flower in her mouth and chewed it up.

On the far side of the pool, buried under creepers and vines, lay the ruins of an ancient temple made of carved stones. Sections of walls had collapsed and much of the structure was hidden by trees that had taken root between the rocks. The boy had explored the temple several times, though he knew it was a place inhabited by snakes and scorpions. A series of steps led down from the broad plinth into the green water and there was a stone channel in the centre, out of which flowed a year-round spring that never went dry, even in the hottest months of summer.

Swimming across the pool, the boy scampered up onto the temple steps and shook himself dry, beads of water spraying out of his long hair in all directions. He knew that the temple had been built by men long ago. The mother elephant had explained to him how human beings constructed walls out of stone by chipping and shaping the rocks and fitting them together. The boy wondered why this building was now empty and covered over by the jungle. Keeping a sharp eye out for poisonous creatures, Mowgli approached the main sanctuary and ran his hands over the walls. They were covered in moss but he could feel the carved shapes and surfaces. Most of the patterns and designs had been worn away over time but he found a few images that he recognized, including the profile of an elephant with its trunk in the air and one foot raised. He also found the carved shape of a water lily, part of which had broken away, though his fingers could still trace the outline of its petals.

Touching these images on the old rocks, the boy became curious about the carvings and the purpose of this ruined building. Human beings must have lived here once, he thought, though they had abandoned the temple long ago. It was now home to many different creatures—bats and lizards, birds that nested in the crevices and hollows, snakes and rats, as well as a porcupine that had burrowed under a pile of rocks, where one of the walls had collapsed.

The matriarch had told the boy many stories about her time in captivity and how she had led processions through the town with drums beating and people dancing in the streets. She had told him about weddings and festivals, how people celebrated and feasted at certain times of the year. Her mahout, Arif Khan, who had trained her when she was young, would tie a bright turban on his head and sit on her neck, the same seat that Mowgli now occupied. Though he carried a sharp goad made of steel, the mahout never beat or threatened her but simply called out commands that she understood, kneeling or raising her trunk, bowing her head and letting children ride on her back. Whenever he heard these stories, the boy felt a strange, unsettling fascination. Though he was curious about life outside the jungle, this was still his home and he felt no desire to leave the sheltering trees and the animals that were his extended family.

As he sat on the temple steps, watching the herd of elephants drinking from the pool, the still surface in front of him suddenly swelled up as the matriarch appeared, spraying water from her trunk. She often submerged herself completely and disappeared beneath the water like a huge fish, swimming down to the bottom of the pool. Now she stood in front of the boy, her dark hide dripping wet and the pink spots, on her face and ears, the colour of a water lily.

Am I really a human? the boy blurted out.

The elephant's eyes studied Mowgli for a moment and he heard the fluttering sound of her breath, like a deep gurgling inside her chest. Sometimes it sounded like a song; rhythmic vibrations that seemed to send ripples across the green water as she replied to his question.

Yes, she said. *And there's nothing wrong with that.*

But then why do I want to live in the jungle forever, instead of going to a village or town? he asked.

Because this is all you've known, the mother elephant replied.

Why did you come back to the forest, after spending so many years amongst men? Mowgli asked her.

I chose to leave, she said, *not because I was unhappy at the Nawab's palace but because I missed the company of my own kind and the freedom of the jungle. Arif Khan, my mahout, was a wise man who understood me better than I knew myself. By the time I was full grown, he was growing old himself, and he had difficulty climbing onto my back. I used to steady him with my trunk but I could feel that he was getting weaker and less agile. Both of us knew that someday soon he would have to hand me over to one of the younger mahouts.*

But then, one morning, we went into the forest to gather leaves and as he guided me into the trees, we came upon a herd of wild elephants that were watching us from a distance. I could hear them calling out to me, not with the words of men but with voices that I recognized from when I was a calf. Arif Khan was nearly deaf by then but he could hear them too, just as you can understand my stories, Mowgli. We were at the edge of the jungle, only a short distance from the town. My mahout ordered me to kneel and when I did, he slid off my back and stroked my ears with one hand. Loosening the rope around my neck, he removed the brass bell at my throat.

'Go!' he said. 'You've served me well but now I will send you back to the wild. Go, Mohua! Join your own kind, but never forget me.'

Both of us had tears in our eyes as Arif Khan turned and walked away, looking back only once to wave a hand and to make sure that I understood. As soon as he was gone, the wild elephants came and welcomed me, leading the way into the forest, where I've lived ever since.

The boy could see emotions welling up in the mother elephant's eyes as she remembered that moment of farewell and her return to the jungle. He wondered if he would ever feel a desire to join his own kind. Mowgli was about to ask something more, when he heard a rock dislodged nearby. It fell into the water with a splash. Looking over his shoulder, he saw that the troop of langurs had arrived at the temple and Chutku was sitting on one of the ruined walls nearby. Leaping to his feet, the boy ran to greet him, waving both arms in excitement.

TEN

As the afternoon light began to fade and shadows grew longer, Mowgli and Chutku climbed into a large banyan tree near the forest pool. It had plenty of comfortable branches and seemed the perfect place to spend the night. They chose a broad saddle between the trunk and one of the spreading limbs. The bark on the tree was as wrinkled and rough as an elephant's hide. As they settled down in the twilight it almost felt as if they were perched atop the matriarch's neck. Both of them felt secure and safe, yawning and blinking their eyes as the sun disappeared beyond a ruffled bank of clouds.

Moments later, however, Mowgli's sixth sense alerted him to danger. He nudged his friend and gestured for him to get up. In the grey-green shadows of the banyan's overlapping branches, they saw a fluid movement at the knotted core of the giant tree. Immediately, Mowgli let out a sharp alarm call that every langur recognizes–a warning that snakes are nearby. Stepping out along the branch, the two friends moved away from the trunk of the tree but as the serpent reached the saddle where they had been seated, it paused and licked the air with its forked tongue. A hamadryade, or king cobra, it was as thick as Mowgli's thigh and four times his length. In the twilit forest the great Naga looked as if one of the branches of the banyan had come to life. Raising its head and spreading its hood, the huge snake fixed its eyes on the boy and the monkey.

From as long ago as he could remember, Mowgli had been terrified of snakes, even the smallest garter snakes that did no one any harm. But this cobra was the largest he had ever seen and he froze with fear, as he stood there, balanced on the branch. Chutku crept further out along the limb. Any courage he might have had to stick by his friend had evaporated the moment he saw the snake's hood open up like a venomous orchid blooming in the dark. Swiftly, the langur leapt off the branch and grabbed onto another limb nearby, swinging himself to safety. Mowgli was now alone and he took a step backwards, arms extended to steady himself. The forest floor was more than fifty feet below him and he knew that if he fell or jumped, he would surely break his neck.

The cobra remained almost motionless for several minutes and the only movement was the flicking of its tongue as if it were tasting the shadows. Finally, Mowgli took another step back, feeling the round shape of the branch beneath his bare feet. He dared not take his eyes off the snake to look behind him. As the boy retreated, he had only his instincts and the nerves in the soles of his feet to guide him. Mowgli had no idea what he would do when he came to a point where the banyan's limb became too thin for him to find a foothold.

By now the other monkeys were repeating the alarm call from trees all around but none of them dared come to his rescue. As he inched away from the snake, Mowgli could see the cobra's eyes reflecting the last rays of the sunset, like two embers glistening in the dark. Slowly, like water flowing along the trunk of the tree, the cobra began to slide forward, its tail slipping over the crook of the branch and coiling up like a vine wrapping around itself. The distance between Mowgli and the snake's hood was less than a couple of strides, though the cautious steps he took backwards were no more than the length of his foot. His splayed toes gripped the branch and several times he felt sure he would slip, though somehow he kept his balance even as his body shook with fear.

Then, all at once, he heard a loud explosion, as if a bolt of lightning had struck nearby. Startled, the boy took another step back but missed his footing and began to fall. At the same moment, he saw the snake turn towards the sound. A second clap of thunder followed the first. Stretching out both arms the boy caught hold of the branch as he fell, grabbing frantically to save himself. Hanging there, clutching the banyan's limb, Mowgli saw the cobra slide away into the knotted heart of the tree. For several moments, he listened but there was only a hollow silence after the two gunshots, as every creature in the forest held its breath and listened.

Finally, when his arms felt as if they were going to give way, Mowgli slowly hoisted himself back onto the branch. Wrapping both legs around the tree limb, he twisted his nimble body and clambered to his feet. Knowing better than to go back into the centre of the tree, he took a couple of running steps and launched himself towards a parallel branch. Now that the cobra had disappeared, he felt new strength and confidence, grabbing one of the banyan's aerial roots that descended almost to the ground. But instead of lowering himself, the boy swung back and forth until he came within reach of another tree nearby, leaping out of the humid shadows of the banyan and onto a safe perch where he knew the cobra would never follow.

Stopping to catch his breath, he could see the familiar silhouettes of langurs in the trees around him. At the same time, Mowgli heard a strange moaning sound that seemed to be coming towards them. By now the jungle lay in darkness though the sky still had a pink aura from the setting sun. Somewhere off to his right, Mowgli heard a langur cough and he recognized the sound immediately. It meant only one thing. A tiger was nearby. Several other monkeys joined in and for a few minutes it sounded as if they were coughing in unison. Opening his eyes as wide as he could, Mowgli scanned the forest floor beneath him, until he saw a curtain of leaves rustling, as if a breeze had stirred the air. Moments later, a large feline shape passed beneath the tree, gliding through the darkness. The moaning sound was coming from the tiger, as if each breath it took was painful. Mowgli gave a cough of alarm and the big cat paused beneath the tree, looking up. The stripes on its coat blended with the shadows and for a moment the tiger seemed to disappear. As it began to move off again, the boy's eyes followed its phantom form. Though the predator's powerful stride was graceful, Mowgli could see that it was limping. Every time it took a step with its left foreleg, the tiger let out a groan of pain.

After the tension subsided, the jungle settled back into its evening torpor, though Mowgli remained wide awake. A few minutes later, Chutku found him sitting on his perch and came across, ashamed of abandoning his friend. They said nothing to each other, listening instead to the night sounds which had a musical rhythm and harmony, the clicking and humming of insects punctuated by the muted call of a moorhen in the pool nearby. Making themselves as comfortable as they could, Mowgli and the langur curled up on the branch for the night.

ELEVEN

Just before dawn, Mowgli woke up to the alarm call of a sambar less than a stone's throw from his perch. The deer's sharp, belling cry made him open his eyes at once, as the alarm was repeated half a dozen times. This was followed by a shriek of surprise from a red junglefowl. Knowing that the tiger must have spent the night nearby, Mowgli decided to investigate.

He was able to work his way across from branch to branch, thirty feet above the ground, until he came in sight of the ruined temple and a thicket of bamboo on one side of the forest pool. Straining his eyes, Mowgli tried to locate where the tiger was lying but he couldn't see any sign of the predator. He listened intently, though the alarm calls had fallen silent. As the day brightened, the crumbling contours of the temple slowly appeared. A flock of jungle babblers began to move about but their calls expressed no anxiety. From all around there was birdsong, a rousing dawn chorus and Mowgli wondered if the tiger had moved off at first light. But as rays of sunshine began to penetrate the forest, his eyes spotted a fiery patch of gold, deep within a bamboo thicket at the base of the temple's plinth. The tiger was still there though it lay as still as a stone. Watching for any movement, the boy wondered if the beast was dead. He was about to let out an alarm call but stopped himself, deciding to hold off and see what happened next.

He didn't need to wait very long, for soon he heard footsteps approaching through the dry leaves. By now there was enough daylight to see the columns of trees and shaggy clusters of foliage. The brittle rustling of leaf litter betrayed the approach of another creature, though Mowgli wasn't sure what it was. He sniffed the air but no breeze was stirring to carry a scent.

Curious to see more of the tiger, he crept across to another branch from where he could just make out the long tail stretched out between a latticework of bamboo. The gold and black patch he had seen was the tiger's haunch and he could now trace its shape through the veil of green leaves surrounding the ancient temple. He wondered if the gunshot had inflicted a fatal wound that had killed the tiger during the night. The tail remained motionless.

On the brown leaves below, Mowgli could see dark splashes of blood. Moments later, a poacher emerged from behind a wild hedge of ber bushes, followed by a second figure—the same two men who had captured the pangolin a couple of days earlier. Holding his gun in both hands, the man stepped forward cautiously, glancing first at the ground and then at the dense foliage ahead. He and his companion were following the blood trail. Though they wore no shoes, their bare feet made the leaves crackle with each step. The poachers were less than fifty feet from the tiger, which still appeared to be dead. Mowgli held his breath, wondering if he should warn the men or the tiger. One creature seemed as dangerous as the other. Then, out of the corner of his eye, the boy saw the tail twitch. It was hardly a movement, more like the blink of an eyelash but he knew the huge cat was alive.

The two men crept forward, stooping under a looped vine and examining another splash of blood on the ground. Neither of them said a word or made a sound, except for the crisp murmur of leaves crushed under their weight. But then, just as the boy was about to sound an alarm, he heard a gruff, throaty moan and saw the tiger charge out of the bamboo. By this time, the armed man was so close that the predator leapt upon him in a single bound and the poacher didn't have a chance to fire his gun. Mowgli gripped the tree trunk in terror, as he saw the tiger lunge forward and sink his teeth into the man's throat. The second poacher, who wasn't armed, let out a scream of terror and turned on his heels, racing back into the jungle, while his companion dropped his gun. After a moment or two the tiger's victim stopped struggling and lay lifeless in the predator's grasp.

Mowgli had seen death many times before but never as sudden or as brutal as the tiger's kill. With a shake of its huge head, the cat dropped the man and looked around. By now there was enough light for the boy to see a wound on the tiger's left shoulder, a bloody gash where last night's bullet had grazed his flesh. Limping, the tiger took a few steps and then lay down, turning to lick the wound with his tongue. Mowgli had been holding his breath and finally let it out, making a soft sigh as he exhaled. Immediately, the tiger looked up into the tree and spotted the boy. As their eyes met, Mowgli felt a combination of fear and aggression pass between them. While he had no sympathy for the dead poacher, the boy knew that this tiger recognized him as an enemy and if he were not safely seated high above the ground, he would have suffered the same fate as the man who lay spreadeagled in the dry leaves.

Though the forest was hushed immediately after the kill, a few tentative alarm calls started up again. A barking deer began to yelp nearby. Peacocks wailed their reedy cries. The sambar, which had moved off, belled once or twice, while a flock of babblers who had stumbled on the tiger and his victim, while foraging in the leaves, flew off with a medley of anxious chatter. The tiger ignored them all. Rising to his feet, after licking his wound, he went across to the pool and drank his fill. Mowgli could hear the slurping of his tongue as the tiger slaked his thirst. Returning to the kill, the predator looked up at the boy once again, as if considering the possibility of climbing the tree. But then, with another shake of his head, he grabbed the dead man by the scruff of his neck and carried him away into the jungle, far out of sight.

It was only then that the rest of the langurs appeared, creeping towards Mowgli with cautious movements. Chutku was among them and the boy could hear the monkeys cooing and murmuring among themselves, as if trying to reassure each other. When they spotted Mowgli sitting by himself, they hurried across to see if he was all right.

What happened? one of the older langurs asked, brushing the boy's hair away from his eyes.

A tiger.... Mowgli said, under his breath.

I know, the langur replied, studying the fear in the boy's eyes. *But what did you see? What did the tiger do?*

He killed the poacher who wounded him last night, Mowgli replied, a tremor in his voice. *It took only a moment or two. The tiger charged from that clump of bamboo and broke the man's neck with his jaws. Then he dragged him away.*

Now, he will eat him, the old langur said with a scowl, as Chutku crawled closer and wrapped an arm around the boy's waist. *He will taste human flesh, just as he has tasted deer and wild boar, as well as our kind, and he will lose his fear of man.*

The tiger saw me, sitting here, the boy said, tears forming in his eyes. *He recognized who I was. I could see that he hates me.*

The old langur shook his head. *No. He doesn't hate you. His fear has turned into something else, not anger but an instinct to protect himself and feed his hunger. Until the hunter's bullet injured him, he kept away from the scent of those like you.*

I don't smell like a man, Mowgli protested.

The old langur sniffed and smiled. *No matter how often you bathe in the river or roll in the dust, you still carry the stench of your species. Most of us can't smell ourselves but don't ever imagine that others aren't able to smell you.*

What's that? Chutku asked, pointing at something that looked like a long stick on the ground.

Before any of the monkeys could stop him, Mowgli quickly slid halfway down the trunk of the tree, peering about to make sure the tiger was nowhere in sight.

His heart was thumping in his chest and his mouth felt as if he'd just bitten into a raw jamun that made his tongue pucker up and go dry. Leaping down onto the carpet of dry leaves, he scuttled across and grabbed the poacher's gun with one hand, then raced back into the tree. The langurs instinctively drew away from the boy, afraid of this weapon. Mowgli too was nervous but once he had regained his perch, he laid the gun across his lap and examined it carefully. Part of it was made from wood that was carved and polished. The rest was fashioned out of smooth steel, a dark blue colour, almost black. For most of its length, the gun had two long stems connected together, side by side. Holding it up, the boy peered into the barrels trying to see what they contained. He could smell an oily, sooty odour as the hard steel slipped between his fingers. More than once, Mowgli had seen how men held the gun to their shoulder and he did the same, raising it and taking aim at the langurs, then laughing as they jumped aside.

TWELVE

A violent cracking of branches and tumult of leaves announced the arrival of the elephant herd. Several young tuskers with sharp ivory spikes jutting out from either side of their trunks, pushed their way through the underbrush, then sidled over to the waterhole to drink, followed by a more sedate procession of mothers, sisters, and aunts. The temple spring in the forest was one of the few year-round sources of water, other than the river, which lay on the far side of the park. Mowgli and the langurs watched from above as the herd paraded into view and made their way to the marshy pool. Soon there was a ring of elephants sucking water into their trunks and spraying it into their mouths. The matriarch was one of the last to emerge from the jungle. Peering up into the tree, she spotted the boy.

What's that in your hands? she asked in a disapproving voice.

A gun.... Mowgli replied.

The mother elephant reached up with her trunk and took the weapon away.

Where did you find it? she demanded.

Mowgli began to explain how the poacher had wounded the tiger and then was attacked. The elephant waved the gun back and forth in her trunk as if she were going to throw it away.

Is the tiger nearby? the matriarch asked.

I don't know, Mowgli replied, pointing behind him. *He went somewhere in that direction.*

You shouldn't be playing with guns, the elephant said sternly. *They're dangerous. You might injure yourself or someone else.*

I wasn't playing with it, Mowgli insisted. *I was just...trying to figure out how it works. Can I have it back, please?*

The mother elephant shook her head solemnly. *No, Mowgli, this isn't a game.*

I promise I won't use it, the boy pleaded. *I'll put it away in a safe place.*

The mother elephant raised her trunk with the gun pointing towards the sky.

The best thing to do with one of these is to break it in two, she told him.

Please don't, the boy begged her. *It's mine!*

No, it isn't, the elephant said. *All you did was find it and pick it up off the ground. That doesn't mean it's yours.*

Yes, but... Mowgli began to argue. *I'm going to hide it away and keep it, in case I need it some day....*

The mother elephant glared at him sternly. *Why would you need it?*

To...to...defend myself, he said.

From what? she asked.

From...the tiger! Mowgli cried.

The elephant eyed the boy suspiciously, noticing the vulnerable expression on his face. He looked so thin and weak, compared to the young tuskers who had finished drinking and were now sparring with each other. The matriarch could imagine how easily a tiger might catch the boy and clamp his jaws around his neck, then shake him like a mouse.

Do you promise you won't use the gun, unless you really have to? she asked.

The boy nodded.

And you'll put it safely away where nobody else can find it?

Again Mowgli's head bobbed up and down.

If I ever see you playing with this again, the elephant warned him, *I'll stamp on it and bend it out of shape, then throw it in the pond.*

Mowgli smiled as the mother elephant handed the gun back to him, stretching out her trunk and placing it in his hands.

Clutching the weapon to his chest, the boy clambered across to a branch that bent down with his weight and lowered him to the ground. With the herd of elephants around, he wasn't afraid of the tiger and he darted across to the ruined temple on the far side of which lay a pile of stones where a section of the shrine had collapsed. Mowgli knew there was an abandoned porcupine's den amongst the rocks, where he had hidden more than once. Squeezing through the entrance, he found himself in a dark, dry cave. It was long enough for the gun to fit inside and he carefully laid it on a shelf of stones.

Emerging from the temple ruins, Mowgli glanced around to make sure that nobody had seen where he'd been but the elephants were too busy drinking water and the langurs had wandered off in search of food. Running across to the pool, Mowgli waded in up to his waist and drank his fill, cupping both hands and letting the water dribble down his chin as he swallowed deeply, until his belly was full. Letting out a satisfied belch, he climbed onto the mother elephant's back.

Soon afterwards, the herd set off in an easterly direction, crossing a couple of dry water channels and entering the core area of the park, where there were no roads or rest houses, only a dense tract of jungle. The elephants barged through tangled webs of creepers and vines, stopping now and then to feed on trees or shrubs that caught their eye. Eventually, they came to a broad valley with an open grassland and a seasonal stream flowing through the middle. It was as wild and remote a place as any in the park. Even the forest guards seldom came here. As they entered the tall grass, which grew higher than the matriarch's shoulders, Mowgli could see only a few feet ahead. Suddenly, out of the grass in front of them appeared the large tusker.

The mother elephant greeted the bull with a fluttering sound and raised her trunk as the male responded by wrapping his trunk around hers in a gesture of affection. Though the tusker lived on his own he joined the herd from time to time. His huge ivory tusks flared out from both sides of his mouth. After a few minutes, he reached up with his trunk and sniffed Mowgli from head to toe. Though the matriarch was the oldest member of the herd and the tops of her ears were folded over, the tusker was almost the same age and his forehead was scarred from battles with other bull elephants though he could be as gentle as a newborn calf. Mowgli saw that the musth fluids, which sometimes oozed from his temples, were not visible which meant he was at peace with the world. There were times, however, when the tusker was in musth and he raged through the forest while everyone stayed out of his way for fear of being trampled.

As the herd carried on through the high grass, Mowgli could see rustling movements all around him, though the other elephants were hidden from view. A little further on, they came to a stretch of sand and rocks that funnelled up into one end of the valley. A stream trickled through the rocks and the elephants stopped to take a sip. Playfully sucking in a snoutful of water, the big tusker sprayed it at Mowgli, soaking his long, tangled hair.

Further ahead lay a grove of bel trees, a favourite delicacy of the herd. The younger ones rushed forward and began to pick the hard, round fruit and stuff it in their mouths. Some of the fruit were as big as Mowgli's head. By the time the tusker and the matriarch reached the grove, most of the low-hanging fruit had been finished off by the others but there was plenty higher up and the tusker reached overhead and plucked several that were out of reach of the younger elephants. He also pulled a branch down, so the matriarch could eat her fill. Scrambling up to the top of the tree, Mowgli broke the fruit and tossed them down. He knew that the skin of the bel fruit was too hard for him to break open, but the matriarch crushed one beneath her foot and handed it to the boy. Scooping out the sweet yellow flesh with his hands, Mowgli gorged on the fruit, until his whole face was sticky with the juice. Sliding down the matriarch's trunk, the boy scampered across to the stream to rinse his fingers and face.

As he ran back to the mother elephant, Mowgli saw that she had raised her trunk and was sniffing the air. Something was wrong. Grabbing the matriarch's tail, he scrambled up over her broad hips and across her back to regain his seat on her neck. The tusker too had raised his trunk and Mowgli could see his nostrils quivering, trying to identify and locate a scent. The boy took a deep breath as well but all he could smell was the sour, grassy odour of the herd.

With an impatient snort, the tusker headed up a nearby slope that ascended a steep escarpment, overlooking the valley. There was no path but he pushed his way through the dry brush and into the trees. The mother elephant and the others followed, clearing a route for themselves as they traversed the slope and finally reached a gulley that led to the top of the ridge. Mowgli was glad to be seated where he was. There weren't enough trees to go from branch to branch and if he'd been on foot it would have taken him three times as long while his arms and legs would have been scratched with thorns. Though the elephants were huge, flat-footed creatures, they were able to move silently through the jungle when they wanted.

At the top of the ridge, they eased themselves forward until they came to a point where they could look down the other side. When Mowgli inhaled again, he could finally smell what the elephants had already sensed.

There was smoke in the air!

THIRTEEN

Stealthily, the elephants moved along the forested contours of the ridge and descended to a point where they could see the upper end of the hidden valley. From his vantage point on the matriarch's neck, Mowgli immediately spotted wisps of smoke rising out of a clearing some distance away. During the dry months of summer, the forest often caught fire and the animals would flee in terror but now the jungle was green and moist. Mowgli had often seen feathery plumes of smoke beyond the edges of the park, rising from village homes, where men set wood and straw alight for their own mysterious purposes.

Slipping forward like great, grey shadows amongst the trees, the elephants were as silent as clouds, circling down to investigate the source of the smoke. When they were just above the streambed, Mowgli saw a couple of tents and several crude huts made of bamboo.

A poacher's camp, the mother elephant whispered. *This is where the men who wounded the tiger must have come from. These are bandits—dacoits. After they finish robbing villages and towns nearby, they sneak into the park and hide, killing animals to eat, while hunting for skins and ivory to sell.*

Ivory? Mowgli asked. *What good is that to them?*

It is as precious as the gold and silver they steal from men, the matriarch replied. *Who knows what purpose it serves except for a bull elephant who wants to show off his strength and self-importance?*

She looked across at the huge tusker and caught his eye.

You seem to know an awful lot about ivory, he mumbled under his breath. *Even if you don't have any tusks yourself.*

The matriarch flapped her ears in irritation.

I didn't live in captivity with human beings for most of my life without learning something of their ways, she answered.

How can you be sure these men are dacoits? the tusker demanded.

Shaking her head the matriarch explained: *When I was a young elephant, living in the custody of the Nawab, the dacoits attacked his palace. They were carrying burning torches and firing guns in the air. Three of us were in the stables and we broke down the doors and charged at the men, scattering them in all directions. I still have a bullet lodged in my skin from that night. Here, Mowgli, you can feel it.*

With her trunk she guided the boy's hand to a spot behind her left shoulder where Mowgli touched a round ball, the size of a litchi seed, over which her thick skin had healed.

I carry it as a reminder, the matriarch said. *Every instinct in my body tells me that those men, camped over there, belong to a criminal gang that steals from the jungle as well as the towns.*

The tusker snorted. *I'm not afraid of them. We've chased off poachers before. If we went into their camp we could trample their tents and uproot their huts before they could reach for their guns.*

No, the mother elephant said. *Better to stay away and leave them alone.*

As she turned, the rest of the herd stepped aside to let her pass and then followed her back up the ridge and down the other side to the sloping grasslands. After they had been walking for a while, Mowgli looked around and noticed that the tusker was not among them, having wandered off on his own once again. Most of the time, the lone bull preferred his own company, roaming wherever he chose.

Beyond the grasslands, they crossed a motor road where Mowgli and the elephants came upon a troop of rhesus monkeys. Unlike his friends, the langurs, these were macaques, a smaller, scruffier animal with ruddy brown fur. Altogether, there must have been twenty adults in the troop, as well as a dozen infants clinging to their mothers' breasts. The rhesus monkeys made way for the elephants, eyeing them with suspicion. They were feeding on the nuts of bauhinia vines, breaking open the large seedpods with their hands. Seeing Mowgli seated on the elephant's back, a couple of them bared their teeth and grunted at him. They knew the boy had grown up within the troop of langurs and these brown monkeys had a longstanding grudge against their silver-haired cousins.

Several weeks ago, they had fought a pitched battle with the langurs over a patch of wild ber bushes. At this time of the year, these thorny shrubs were covered with ripe fruit, one of Mowgli's favourites. The rhesus macaques had been gorging themselves when the langurs arrived and tried to chase them off. Watching from a distance, Mowgli and Chutku had seen the two bands of monkeys attack each other, screaming and snarling viciously. One of the younger langurs had been bitten by a large male macaque but eventually they were able to scare off the brown monkeys and eat their fill. Remembering the sweet, crisp flavour of the ber fruit, Mowgli's mouth began to water.

He recognized that of all the creatures in the jungle, he was more akin to the monkeys than to any of the other animals, even the elephants. As Mowgli watched the rhesus troop, he could see how similar their faces were to his, their eyes and noses and the way they nibbled on fruit or seeds. At the same time, he felt an immediate sense of animosity because of his loyalty to the langurs. It was strange, he thought, that two species of animals so similar to each other wouldn't get along. Maybe it was because they competed for the same kind of food and occupied the same trees.

FOURTEEN

Several days after Mowgli and the elephants spotted the poacher's camp, the herd was browsing on a low hill covered with bamboo. While the others stuffed their mouths with trunkfuls of fresh leaves, Mowgli broke off the new shoots sprouting at the base of a thicket and peeled away the outer layers, eating the tender core. Bamboo shoots weren't his favourite food but the mild, nutty flavour satisfied the boy's appetite. As he was chewing contentedly, Mowgli noticed vultures circling in the sky some distance away. He understood that the big birds gathered whenever an animal died, which often happened in the forest, whether it was a predator's kill, or other natural causes. Mowgli knew that life and death were part of the continuous cycle of the jungle, though the thought of eating dead meat, as the vultures did, filled him with revulsion.

A little while later, he heard the rumbling sound of two vehicles passing along a dirt track that circled the foot of the hill. Through a curtain of trees, he saw a group of forest guards in two jeeps heading in the direction of the vultures. Usually, Mowgli wouldn't have paid much attention to the passing vehicles but for some reason an uneasy premonition came over him and he wondered if the tiger had killed again.

The matriarch also noticed the vultures and once the herd had gorged itself on bamboo, she led them down to find out what had happened. The circling birds were a long way off and the elephants moved at a slow, sedate pace, pausing now and then to pluck a tasty bunch of leaves or to sniff at a jackal's burrow or a termite castle that had been dug up by a bear. Each animal had its own tastes. Mowgli wondered what it must be like to eat ants, though his tongue itched at the thought. Maybe if he was hungry enough, though right now his stomach was full.

As they drew closer, a rotting stench filled the air. At first it was very faint but when they came within range of the wheeling birds, it grew stronger and stronger, until the boy covered his nose with one hand. By now, he could sense anxiety in the herd. Rushing forward, the matriarch impatiently pushed her way through the undergrowth, trampling bushes and uprooting saplings that stood in her path. Even before they reached the dry riverbed, Mowgli knew that something terrible had happened. The sandy watercourse was littered with round rocks while tufts of tall grass grew along the edges.

From a distance, they saw the two jeeps parked beside what looked like a large grey boulder. Mowgli crouched behind the mother elephant's head so he couldn't be seen but as soon as the forest guards caught sight of the approaching herd, they retreated to their vehicles and drove off in a hurry. By now, Mowgli had recognized the dead tusker. He lay on his side, facing away from them. As the jeeps departed, three of the vultures descended, landing on top of the bull elephant. Charging forward the herd chased them away and encircled the corpse to protect it from scavengers. Mowgli could feel the matriarch's body trembling beneath him, the anxious fluttering of her breath vibrating like leaves quivering in the air before a storm. The boy himself was shaking now for he could see bullet holes in the elephant's shoulder and side, as well as one in the temple, a trickle of blood flowing down the dead elephant's cheek. Through a film of tears, Mowgli saw with horror that the bull's ivory tusks had been hacked away and removed, leaving two gaping wounds.

A chorus of grief arose from the herd, a pained, moaning sound so low and deep that Mowgli could barely hear it though he could feel it rumbling within the matriarch's throat. All the elephants were weeping together, their eyes streaming with tears and their bodies swaying from side to side in a mournful rhythm. One by one, they began to pick up the round river rocks with their trunks and place them on and around the corpse. Slowly but deliberately, the herd covered the lifeless body with stones, piling them up like a mountain.

Most of the rocks were white or pale grey, all of them polished by centuries of monsoon floods. With their huge feet, the elephants pried boulders loose from the sand and rolled them onto the grave. Except for the eerie song that emanated from deep within their lungs, they made no other sounds. Mowgli too slid down from the matriarch's neck and began to gather stones from the riverbed to add to the cairn.

By nightfall, the tusker's body was completely covered by a heap of rocks. Each of the elephants placed a final stone on the burial mound and then formed a circle around the tomb. Throughout the night, they stood vigil by the tusker's grave, singing their solemn dirge as the stars turned in the heavens and the moon appeared, bathing the forest in its creamy light so that the heap of boulders shone like ivory. In the lunar aura, tears continued to flow down the creases of the matriarch's wrinkled cheeks. A procession of animals came to pay their respects. The first to arrive was the troop of langurs, who took up position in the trees nearby. Next came a herd of chital deer that slipped out of the shadows, their dappled coats shimmering in the moonlight, followed by barasingha with branching antlers. Jungle cats and jackals, porcupines and hyenas, even a pack of dhole made an appearance. A sloth bear and his mate lumbered by, rising up on their hind legs for a minute and then shambling on, followed by a delegation of wild boar. Two panthers crept out of the tall grass and circled the burial mound before slinking away into the dark margin of trees. The tusker had lived in the forest longer than any of the others and there wasn't an animal who hadn't encountered his benevolent presence. Even when he was in musth, he had been a gentle rogue. As Mowgli's eyes grew heavy, he watched the mourners come and go without a sound, barking deer and martens, sambar and nilgai, each in turn. They all came and listened to the elephants' lament, cocking their ears to the sound and then lowering their heads. Eventually, though, when all the creatures had departed and the moonlight seemed to cast a pale shroud over the tusker's grave, Mowgli saw a familiar shape detach itself from the dark silhouettes of the trees and move across the dry riverbed with a fluid yet powerful gait, despite a limp in one leg. The boy was about to scramble up onto the matriarch's shoulders but clutched the inside of her foreleg instead.

The tiger kept his distance, standing in the moonlight and observing the elephants' rituals from afar. He and the lone tusker had fought more than once but in recent years they had reached a truce and kept away from each other out of mutual respect. Now that his old adversary was gone, the tiger seemed to pause in solemn remembrance, his tail waving from side to side, his striped fur colourless in the bleached light of the moon. And then he was gone.

It was only hours later, when dawn began to paint a pale glow in the sky and the moon disappeared behind the treetops that the herd fell silent at last, their bass chorus dissipating with the night as they swayed together in mourning, the forest funeral complete. Much earlier, Mowgli had fallen asleep in the soft sand between the matriarch's feet but he felt her trunk nudging him awake, then lifting him up onto her back, as the herd began to move off, departing into the jungle as the first rays of sunlight gilded the tusker's grave.

Riding on the mother elephant's back, Mowgli wondered if all the animals he'd seen during the night had been part of a dream, especially the tiger drifting away into the shadows. The herd moved quickly now with a steady sense of purpose. None of them, not even the youngest, most mischievous bulls, paused to grab a leaf or a mouthful of grass, marching behind the matriarch.

When they came to the forest pool near the ruined temple, nobody stopped to take a drink, heads held high and their strides unwavering. Mowgli glanced around nervously, then jumped to the ground, hurriedly scampering up the stone steps to the top of the temple plinth, where the walls of the shrine were wrapped in roots. Darting to the back of the ruins, he reached the entrance to the porcupine's den and squeezed through a gap in the rocks. Grabbing the poacher's gun, he dragged it behind him as he crawled on hands and knees, emerging into daylight once again.

By now, the last of the elephants were passing by and Mowgli ran to catch up, the heavy gun weighing him down. Grabbing the tail of the last member of the herd, he swung himself up onto her back and then jumped from one to the next, leaping from elephant to elephant and ducking under branches that swung overhead, until he finally reached the matriarch who was leading the way. Out of breath and still trembling with emotion, the boy wedged his feet behind the mother elephant's ears and rested the twin barrels of the gun across his knees.

FIFTEEN

As the solemn procession of elephants marched through the jungle, Mowgli soon realized they were not alone. Many of the animals who had come to the tusker's grave the night before, were now following them through the forest. The langurs travelled atop the trees while between the layers of leaves, Mowgli could see deer keeping pace with the herd. Occasionally, a nilgai or black buck crossed their path, then fell into step. When they reached the grasslands, Mowgli saw the same pair of leopards slip out of the trees to their right. To his left, a barasingha stag and three does emerged from the forest. The animals moved silently in unison, as if a steady gust of wind were blowing through the tall grass.

Examining the gun on his lap, Mowgli could see different parts attached to each other, though he still wasn't sure how it worked. Holding the weapon and sitting on the matriarch's back, he felt braver than he'd ever felt before but also anxious about what might happen next. The bandits would be armed and if they fired their guns some of the elephants and other animals were sure to be injured or killed. He wondered what it must feel like to have a bullet pierce your body. Would it burn like fire? Would it sting like a wasp? Would it ache like a bruise?

Entering the hidden valley, the matriarch held up her trunk to signal silence, though the elephants and other animals hadn't made a sound. They knew that surprise was their best weapon against the poachers though in daylight it would be difficult to avoid being seen. Nevertheless, they reached the edge of the clearing without anyone raising an alarm. The tents and huts lay on the opposite side of a broad meadow. Wood smoke was trailing out of one shelter.

A couple of men were lounging in the sun and Mowgli guessed the others were in their tents. If the animals were to charge across the clearing, the men would have plenty of time to get their guns.

Gesturing again with her trunk, the mother elephant signalled for half of the herd to circle around to the other side. One of the older females took charge of this group as they detached themselves and disappeared into the jungle. Watching them leave, Mowgli noticed a flash of gold on an outcropping of boulders nearby. Moments later, the tiger edged forward and crouched on the rocks, studying the poacher's camp intently. Mowgli instinctively clutched the gun.

Preparations for the attack were in place and each of the animals waited for the matriarch to signal a charge but before she could give the command, a commotion broke out behind them. Mowgli immediately recognized the shrill hoots and screams of the rhesus macaques. The brown monkeys had followed the herd quietly but now began squabbling among themselves. Immediately, the two dacoits stood up, shading their eyes and staring at the trees, while more men came out of the huts with guns in their hands.

Trumpeting loudly, the matriarch now led the charge, thundering out of the trees with the herd at her heels. A sounder of boar erupted from the right and the langurs leapt down from the trees with gruff, booming cries. From every corner of the clearing, an army of animals emerged, sambar and chital stags, even the timid barking deer. On the opposite side of the clearing, the rest of the elephants burst into view, accompanied by bears and hyenas. The dacoits quickly took aim and fired. The animals replied with bellowing and roars, sharp battle cries and fierce snarls of rage as the men hurried to reload their weapons. By now, they were close enough so that Mowgli could see the terrified expressions on the men's faces. He also noticed one of the dacoits, who wore a green woollen cap, raise his gun and aim at the matriarch. Though the boy could barely hold on as the elephant charged, he pointed his gun at the armed man. Struggling to make it fire, he pushed and pulled the different parts on the weapon but nothing happened. A couple more gun shots rang out and bullets buzzed past his ears like beetles zipping through the air. Mowgli squeezed whatever he could find until finally there was a loud bang and he felt the gun leap in his hands, kicking him painfully in the chest and throwing him off the elephant's back. The gun flew out of his hands and Mowgli hit the ground with a thud that knocked the breath from his lungs, as the elephants raced into the centre of the poacher's camp.

A few minutes later, when the boy could finally breathe again, he opened his eyes and looked around. The animals were now rampaging through the camp, uprooting the tents and toppling the bamboo huts. It looked as if the battle was over but then he saw one of the dacoits get to his feet, behind a large termite castle where he had taken shelter. It was the same bandit with the green woollen cap and he had a knife in one hand. Brandishing the long steel blade, he advanced towards Mowgli, revenge in his eyes. The boy looked around desperately but there was no sign of the gun and nothing with which he could defend himself.

He froze where he was, eyes fixed on the man who rushed towards him with the knife. The elephants were too far away and with all the noise and confusion, nobody could hear Mowgli, as he shouted for help. The boy wanted to run but his legs wouldn't move and he was still gasping for breath from his fall, a painful ache in his chest. The bandit was now almost upon him, cursing angrily, though Mowgli couldn't understand a word. Sunlight glinted off the lethal blade.

But then, all at once, the attacker stopped in his tracks. His threatening demeanour changed to a look of fear. It was as if he had seen a ghost, retreating one step backwards...and then another. Finally, with a cry of horror, he pivoted about and started to run. Confused and alarmed, Mowgli turned his head and looked behind him, just as the tiger came racing across the clearing, his mouth wide open and his eyes full of fury.

Mowgli had just enough time to crouch down and cover his head but he felt the fur on the tiger's belly brush against his skin as it leapt over him and chased after the dacoit, who was now running for his life. Feeling his legs give way, the boy dropped to the ground, gasping for breath. He had never been so frightened in his life...or so relieved.

By now the camp had been destroyed and those bandits who weren't able to run away, had climbed a tall shisham tree to escape the herd. Five of them were sitting on the limbs, holding on for their lives, as the elephants violently jostled the tree, shaking it from all sides. Mowgli got up and went across to see what was happening, though his legs still wobbled as he walked. While he didn't seem to have broken any bones, each time he sucked air into his lungs, his ribs hurt.

Chutku was the first to spot him and came racing over to embrace Mowgli, jabbering with excitement. Three of the largest langurs had now climbed into the shisham tree and they began to pelt the dacoits with twigs and sticks, baring their teeth as the men clutched at the branches, their pleading voices crying out in surrender. None of the animals had been seriously injured, though the matriarch had a cut on her forehead and there was a trickle of blood running down her trunk. When she saw Mowgli, she drew him against her protectively. A couple of deer looked as if they'd been shaken up in the fight and one of the stags had a dacoit's torn trousers stuck on his horns. The tiger and leopards had already disappeared. Inside one of the tents, an elephant was rummaging around and let out a loud trumpet of rage. Lifting one of the giant tusks in her trunk, she shook her head and waved it at the men who were clinging to the tree overhead.

Minutes later, Mowgli heard the rumble of jeeps as two vehicles full of forest guards came to a halt at the edge of the clearing. They were carrying guns but came no closer, as the dacoits shouted for help. The animals stood their ground for several minutes, until the matriarch signalled for the herd to follow her into the forest. Mowgli hoisted Chutku onto his back and set off behind two of the elephants that were carrying the dead bull's bloodstained tusks. Soon they were making their way up a slope of the ridge, overlooking the hidden valley. Below them the guards in the jeeps had surrounded the shisham tree as the animals dispersed, each species heading off in its own direction.

⁂

Finally, when they reached the ruined temple, the elephants and langurs stopped to drink at the forest pool. All of them were thirsty and exhausted from the battle. After they finished spraying themselves and drinking their fill, the matriarch beckoned to Mowgli with her trunk.

I need your help, she said in a quiet, serious tone.

The boy nodded.

Will you put these two tusks beneath those rocks, where you hid the gun? You're the only one who can crawl inside.

What do you want to put them there for? Mowgli asked.

We'll bury them, so nobody will ever be able to dig them up.

The elephants helped Mowgli by pushing the tusks through the narrow entrance, while he pulled from inside. Chutku also joined him as the boy struggled under the weight of the ivory. Eventually, they were able to lay the tusks side by side, inside the hidden chamber at the heart of the ruined temple. When they finally emerged, the matriarch and two of the other elephants pushed a boulder in place, sealing the entrance forever.

II
THE FOUNDLING

ONE

253 (M)/1960.6.5/01.AR

Admission Report Date: 6 May 1960

Calvary Mission Children's Home, Shakkarganj, Uttar Pradesh, India

Name: Unknown

Sex: Male

D.O.B & Age: Unknown, approximately 6-7 years

Height: 3 feet 10 inches

Weight: 46 lbs

Family Status: No known relatives

The child was brought to us by two forest guards from the Hathi Talao Wildlife Sanctuary, thirty-six kilometres north-east of Shakkarganj. He was in an emaciated condition, with a severe case of malarial fever and clear evidence of malnutrition and dehydration. From the state of his health and hygiene, the boy appears to have been living on his own for several weeks, possibly months. His hair was long, matted, and infested with lice. His elbows and knees were heavily calloused and there were festering sores on his upper body. The guards reported that he was naked when they found him, lying near a waterhole in a section of the park known as Meethapani Block. There were no injuries on his body or any evidence of physical abuse though his right shoulder was bruised. He was semi-conscious but resisted examination even in his weakened state. Twice he tried to bite me and scratched one of our aides with his fingernails, which were untrimmed and ragged. He did not respond to either Hindustani or English, or any of the local dialects of this region.

With some difficulty we were able to administer an intravenous drip of chloroquine and several other drugs for the fever. His sores were cleaned, and an antibiotic ointment was applied, though he tried to lick it off immediately. We have quarantined him in a storeroom behind the dispensary. Fortunately, Anjali Joseph, one of the nurses from the mission hospital in Amrudpur, happened to be here on her weekly visit, when he was brought in by the forest guards. She agreed to stay back for several days to attend to his condition. At this point, we do not know if he will survive for his body is constantly trembling from the fever and twice he has had what seem to be epileptic fits.

Of course, there has been a lot of speculation, encouraged by the forest guards, that this boy was living in the company of wild animals and he may have been raised by wolves, bears, or monkeys. I have discouraged our staff and children from spreading these rumours. While it might make for a good story by Rudyard Kipling, the truth is that a child of his age would have been more likely to be eaten in the wild by any number of predators, rather than nurtured by some other species. From his appearance and behaviour, he seems to suffer from mental disability and my initial assessment is that his parents, being desperately poor and ill-equipped to deal with his disabilities, found they could no longer care for the boy and abandoned him in the forest. A number of migrant communities, some of them hunters and gatherers, pass through this region, along the foothills of the Himalaya, and it is likely that he comes from one of these nomadic tribes.

We have filed a report with the police in Amrudpur and they will investigate whether any cases of missing children are pending in the district, though it doesn't seem likely and the superintendent of police has given us temporary custody of the boy. In situations like this there is always a lot of paperwork and red tape that must be completed, and I imagine the district magistrate will get involved. In the meantime, our primary objective is to save the boy's life. If he does not respond to medication, we may have to transport him to the hospital in Amrudpur.

The Lord has sent us this foundling and it is our calling to provide succour to the weakest, most wretched and forsaken of His children. As it is written in the Gospels, after Jesus was baptized, 'The Spirit immediately drove him out into the wilderness. And he was in the wilderness forty days, tempted by Satan; and he was with the wild beasts; and the angels ministered to him.' (Mark 1:12-13) But as the prophet Jeremiah proclaimed, 'I will restore health to you and your wounds I will heal, declares the Lord, because they have called you an outcast.' (Jeremiah 30:17)

Signed:

Miss Elizabeth Cranston

Principal

Calvary Mission Children's Home

Shakkarganj

253 (M)/1960.6.5/02.PR　　　　　　　　　14 June 1960

Progress Report

Daniel was christened this morning before the Sunday service. I don't think he understood anything of what took place and he does not respond to his Christian name. Once he reaches an age when he can recognize and appreciate God's love, he will be confirmed and receive communion. Another younger child, Mary, was also christened. She came to us last week, the daughter of lepers who gave her up for fear she would contract their disease. A bright-eyed, cheerful girl of two, she laughed when I sprinkled water on her forehead and seemed to think it was all an innocent joke. I can't help comparing her to Daniel, who has such a wary, unsettled expression on his face and flinches every time I come near him. Two of the aides held him by the arms and brought him to the altar. With a lot of difficulty, we have been able to dress him in a loose smock though he often pulls it off and prefers to be naked. After the baptism he was taken back to his room before I conducted the rest of the service, for he becomes disruptive and the other children begin to laugh and whisper among themselves.

It has taken us a month to gain some level of trust with the boy. For the first week, he could hardly move and the fever made him delusional, tossing about as if in a nightmare. We prayed over him every day and Nurse Joseph helped heal his sores. Once his malaria subsided, he got his appetite back and had no hesitation in eating. We gave him khichri at first and he sniffed it suspiciously, but his preference is for fruit and raw vegetables. He chews on carrots as if they were candy. Last week, we harvested our litchis and he ate so many, he threw up. But it was the mangoes that provided our first breakthrough. Until then, he hadn't let anyone come near him and we had to tie his hands and feet before we could wash him and cut his hair. He struggled violently and the aides were afraid of him but when I brought him a mango from one of the trees behind my bungalow, I could immediately see his expression change and he let me kneel in front of him. Taking the fruit, he eagerly squeezed it with both hands, as if he knew exactly what he was doing, then bit a hole in one end and sucked the juice and pulp. From his gestures, I could tell he'd eaten a mango before and he peeled it with his teeth, licking the skin and seed as if he dared not waste a drop.

After that, every day I have brought him a mango and he no longer cringes in one corner, the way he used to do. He even lets me place my hand on his head while he sucks at the fruit. There is still a kind of wildness about him, what some might call a savage nature, though I can tell it is mostly fear.

I chose the name Daniel because he came to us from the tiger's den. Though it is inconceivable that he was raised by wild beasts, the fact that he was found in the jungle proves that the Lord protected him and delivered him from danger. After choosing his name I went back and read the Book of Daniel. The verses describing King Nebuchadnezzar's dream struck me as prophetic. 'Let him be wet with the dew of heaven; let his lot be with the beasts in the grass of the earth; let his mind be changed from a man's and let a beast's mind be given to him.' (Daniel 4: 15-16)

253 (M)/1960.6.5/03.PR　　　　　　　　　　4 July 1960

Years ago, my parents started a tradition that on every Fourth of July, we will celebrate with fireworks. I tell the children it is America's birthday and they have learned to sing 'The Star-Spangled Banner', though most of them don't understand the words and Samuel accompanies them on the harmonium, which always sounds a little off-key, more like a bhajan than a national anthem.

Daniel joined us for the celebrations and listened attentively to the song, though he did not try to join in or clap his hands to the rhythm. We had cake and jalebis, which he enjoyed, eating with both hands and licking his fingers. The other children are gradually getting used to his presence and sometimes he lets them sit with him and show him the pictures they have drawn or the games they play. I know they call him 'Jungli' behind my back and the older ones snicker when he walks, because he often drops to his knees or scuttles along the ground. An aide remains by his side whenever he's out of his room because we are worried that he may try to run away or hurt someone.

After the cake had been eaten and the sun was going down, I signalled to the older boys that they could light the crackers and bottle rockets. For the younger ones we have sparklers. I was standing close by to make sure that nobody got hurt. When the first rocket went off and a string of crackers exploded, there was a commotion near the water pump and I looked across to see the aides chasing Daniel. The fireworks had terrified him and he had let out a cry of panic. Racing away before anyone could catch him, he climbed into the jacaranda tree beyond the dining hall. I told the boys to stop the fireworks immediately and went across to the tree. It was almost completely dark by now for a monsoon storm was coming in, but I could see him perched in the upper branches and clinging to the trunk of the tree. We could not persuade him to come down and I told the aides not to try and go up after him for fear he might fall. It rained during the night but he stayed up there until dawn and only came down when one of the ayahs brought him his breakfast. Descending slowly, hand over hand; he was still wet and shivering from the storm.

253 (M)/1960.6.5/04.PR   2 August 1960

The monsoon this year has been intermittent, with a few days of heavy rain followed by prolonged periods of heat and humidity that becomes almost unbearable. Adding to our misery, the electricity keeps going off and when the fans stop working, the dormitories become claustrophobic. I have moved my bed up onto the roof, where I now sleep under a mosquito net, though the insects somehow always have a way of getting inside and waking me up by buzzing in my ears.

I mention this because the children too have taken to sleeping on the roof of the dormitory and we sprinkle the bricks on the terrace with water to cool them down each evening. I've erected tents of mosquito netting and six or eight children sleep under one of these canopies, catching a few breezes at night. The only problem is when a sudden monsoon squall arrives, everyone has to scramble indoors with their bedding.

Poor Daniel has been confined to his room because he still isn't ready to stay in the dormitory. Sometimes I feel as if we're locking him up like a prisoner or an untamed animal, but he isn't properly socialized and still needs to develop an understanding of how to live indoors with other children. Sometimes, when the lights go off and the air grows still, I can hear him calling out, a pitiful wailing cry, as if he were pleading for help. It's a sad, unsettling sound and the other night, I finally got up and went down to try and comfort him. When I opened the door of the storeroom, where he stays, there was a strong smell of urine and he was huddled on one corner of the pallet, though he'd wet the rest of his bed.

I took him by the hand and led him out of the room and across to my bungalow, where a brick staircase leads up to the roof. He seems to trust me now and I put a couple of pillows on the ground beside my bed, beneath the mosquito net and let him sleep there. It wasn't long before I could hear his breathing become a murmuring snore. But later, towards dawn, I woke up to hear him making strange sounds in his sleep, muted grunts and snuffling. Peering down from my bed, I could see that he was dreaming, twitching wildly in his sleep. He must have been having a nightmare and I reached over to touch his shoulder, when he woke up abruptly, his eyes wide with fear, staring at me as if I were a terrifying monster from his dreams.

253 (M)/1960.6.5/05.PR   10 September 1960

Soon after I wrote my last report Daniel had a relapse of malaria and he was very sick for a couple of weeks. In fact, I thought we were going to lose him. He was admitted to the hospital in Amrudpur and the doctors there were finally able to bring the fever under control. He is back with us now and much better, though still weak and almost as thin as he was when he first arrived. Yesterday, I received a notice from the district magistrate's office informing us that the police have been unable to trace his family and that there is no report of a missing child corresponding to his age or description. They have, therefore, authorized us to keep him here as an orphan, which means that he is now, officially, our responsibility.

Following his recovery from the second bout of fever, Daniel seems calmer and less anxious than before. He allows the aides and ayahs to bathe and dress him. His hair, which we shaved off because it was crawling with lice, has grown back enough to comb and part. In his uniform, he looks very civilized, though he remains aloof from most of the other children and still has a distracted, unsettled look about him, as if he is not yet reconciled to his new surroundings. He seems to be growing attached to one of the ayahs, Shanti, who has taken a special interest in him.

One of the things I have discovered is that Daniel is a remarkable mimic. The other day, as I was walking by the dispensary, a koel was calling from the mango trees nearby. Suddenly, I heard what sounded like a second bird answering the first and I looked around to try and spot it. After a minute or two, I realized that it was Daniel. He gets the pitch right, a mournful whistle that has a haunting tone. Later on, I heard him imitating several other birds, including a crow making hoarse cawing sounds and pigeons cooing on the windowsills.

253 (M)/1960.6.5/06.PR   6 October 1960

Daniel is doing remarkably well and seems to be adjusting to his new home. Last week, we were able to move him out of his temporary quarters in the storeroom next to the dispensary and he has been given a bed in the boy's dormitory. The other children still treat him with caution but he has made friends with Pradeep, who is a little younger than him and has a lame leg. I have seen them playing together and the other day, Daniel was carrying Pradeep around on his back, which surprised us all because only six months ago, he wouldn't let anyone touch him.

Earlier, I had assumed that he was mentally retarded but I'm not so sure any more. There is a vacant look in his eyes sometimes and his movements make it seem as if he is disabled; a fidgety manner that suggests there has been some brain damage, perhaps from the fever and malnutrition. But at the same time, he is proving himself to be a bright boy. In my last report, I mentioned his mimicry, which continues. He is particularly good at imitating Shanti Ayah, who has a high-pitched giggle that is irrepressible when she is amused. Daniel has taken to copying her and it sets them both off in hysterical laughter. Often, the other children join in. Yesterday, in the dining hall, he started and soon everyone was laughing. I came in to see what was going on and Daniel looked quite pleased with himself, being the instigator of this merriment. In moments like this, I always recall the words of our Saviour: 'Let the children come to me, and do not hinder them; for to such belongs the kingdom of heaven.' (Matthew 19: 13)

253 (M)/1960.6.5/07.PR 5 December 1960

On Sunday we had an incident with Daniel, which made me realize that though he is making significant progress, a number of questions still remain unanswered, both about his past and the future which lies ahead of him. He attends chapel now as well as our Sunday service, sitting silently beside his friend, Pradeep. Whether he understands that this is a time of worship, I can't say, but he usually restrains himself and sits still in his seat.

However, while I was praying after the first hymn, a cat wandered into the chapel, through a side door to the right of the pulpit. It is one of the compound creatures, a scruffy, half-wild tomcat that lives in the ruins of the old sugar mill. Daniel had seen it several times before and Shanti told me that he was afraid of the cat, in a way he hasn't been with the dogs, cows, and goats that wander about. For some reason, the cat set him off, possibly because the old tom was carrying a dead sparrow in his mouth. I was in the middle of prayer, with my eyes closed, so I didn't notice what was going on, but as soon as the cat started down the aisle, Daniel became agitated and stood up. He was making a low, mumbling cry, somewhere between a moan and a sigh. It was one of the strangest noises I've heard, unlike any other sound a person or an animal would make. When I opened my eyes, I saw Daniel leaping over the other children in his row, knocking down chairs and scattering hymnals, as the cat calmly strolled by. Amos and David, two of the aides, got up to control him, but Daniel bit Amos on the wrist when he tried to catch him, then ran out the door, still making a howling noise.

Ending my prayer abruptly, I stopped the service and asked the children to pick up the chairs and then stay in their seats. Going outside the chapel, I looked around for Daniel but he was nowhere in sight. The staff were attending the service but I asked one of the aides and a chowkidar to go and try to find him. Returning to the chapel, I resumed our worship, though I could tell that everyone in the congregation—both children and adults—were alarmed and unsettled.

When we finished, I checked to see if Daniel had been found but there was no sign of him. The aides and ayahs searched everywhere. There is a wall around the compound, though it's easy enough to climb over. Also, the main gates weren't locked. I thought that maybe Daniel would appear for lunch because he is often the first to line up and knows exactly when meals are served, even before the bell is rung. But when one of the senior boys clanged the gong to call everyone to lunch, Daniel did not appear.

As the afternoon stretched into evening, I began to get more worried and sent three groups out to search for him. The village of Shakkarganj lies immediately to the south of us and a couple of aides went to find out if anyone had seen the boy. There are sugarcane fields to the north and east of the compound. These hadn't been harvested yet, standing almost ten feet tall and dense as bamboo thickets. Beyond the fields lies a dry streambed that fills with water during the monsoon and on the far side is a patch of scrub jungle at the foot of a low ridge.

One of the search parties crossed the streambed and cast about, calling Daniel's name. Among them was Shanti Ayah. She told me afterwards that they were about to give up because it was growing dark when she heard a soft wailing sound coming from a clay bank at the edge of the scrub jungle. It was here that they found Daniel, crouching under the exposed roots of a tree, where he'd found a hiding place. Reluctantly, he let Shanti take his hand and lead him back to the compound. Though I am relieved that Daniel is safe and seems to be settling back into his routines, his strange behaviour and terror of cats made me wonder what might have imprinted those fears in his mind. There is a residual wildness about him that reminds me of Ezekiel's lamentation: 'He prowled among lions; he became a young lion, and he learned to catch prey; he devoured men.' (Ezekiel 19: 6)

253 (M)/1960.6.5/08.PR 15 February 1961

Daniel spoke his first word today and it was a remarkable moment that made us all proud of him. He and his constant companion, Pradeep, were in the dining hall, being served their midday meal. One of the aides helps them because Pradeep has trouble managing a tray on his own while using a crutch and Daniel still hasn't mastered serving himself without spilling, though he tries his best. When they sat down at the table, the aide asked them if they wanted water and Daniel immediately chimed in with the word, 'paani'. The aide was so startled he didn't think he had heard him correctly but when he brought them each a tumbler of water, Daniel repeated 'paani', with a knowing look.

There is no question that he is an intelligent boy and I have been waiting for this moment for some time now, but the fact that he is beginning to speak Hindustani, less than a year after his arrival, is gratifying. Now that he understands the concept of language, I think he will pick it up quickly. I have seen him listening attentively to the other children and it is clear that he wants to be a part of their games and activities, though he has a long way to catch up. Fortunately, his health has improved considerably since the last bout of malaria and he has put on fifteen pounds along with gaining a couple of inches in height. Daniel has also learned basic hygiene and bathes himself at the tube well. He also uses the latrine rather than soiling and wetting his bed or relieving himself in the garden as he used to do.

Unlike many of the children that we take in, Daniel has

a natural resilience and an independent streak, what could be called a survival instinct. He has the wits to look after himself and seems to know what's edible and what isn't. His relationship with Pradeep is intriguing for he obviously recognizes his friend's disability and understands the need to cooperate and collaborate with others. On the surface, this may seem a minor issue but when I think about how distrustful and defensive he was when the forest guards brought him here, I realize that he must have been badly traumatized in addition to being seriously ill. The healing process for him has been slow and incremental but it reveals characteristics or traits he acquired from before...who knows how or from where.

253 (M)/1960.6.5/09.PR   2 May 1961

The Lord has surely blessed us with Daniel's presence. In the year that we have had him in our midst he has taught us patience and given us a new appreciation for all that we possess. This morning, I found myself praying: 'Our Heavenly Father, you have brought this boy amongst us for a purpose that we may not comprehend, but we are grateful for the challenges he has brought with him as well as his innocent ways. Too often we take for granted the mastery of tasks that Daniel is still unable to perform. Through the changes we see in him and through his process of learning we gain a greater understanding of Your love and compassion.'

During chapel this morning, as I was leading the children in The Lord's Prayer, I could see Daniel's lips moving, as if he were speaking the words with us: 'Our Father who art in heaven, hallowed be thy name...' Of course, he cannot speak or understand English, and his Hindustani amounts to a limited vocabulary of thirty or forty words that he still can't put together as sentences. Nevertheless, I feel he has absorbed the meaning of what is being said and the Holy Spirit enters him the way it entered the people at the time of Pentecost, letting them speak in tongues.

Every day now, I bring Daniel to the bungalow for an hour

to work with him individually. He is a bright, inquisitive boy and I speak to him mostly in English to help him get an ear for the language. He has picked up a few English words like 'book' and 'chair' but mostly he speaks Hindustani. We usually sit in my office and he is fascinated by the objects on my desk, particularly a small elephant, carved out of ivory. It was a gift my mother gave me when I was twelve or thirteen and I've kept it ever since. She told me once that she bought it from a second-hand curio shop in Mussoorie and had no idea where it came from originally. Soon after he started coming to the house for lessons, the elephant caught Daniel's eye and he pointed at it insistently, until I took it down and let him hold it in his hands. Now, every time he comes for his lessons, I let him touch the miniature elephant, as if it were a ritual. He is very gentle with it and strokes it with his fingers. I tried to teach him the word 'elephant' but he had trouble pronouncing it, though when I gave him the Hindustani word 'hathi', he repeated it immediately. As I try to teach Daniel to speak, I think of the words of the prophet Isaiah: 'The Lord GOD has given me the tongue of those who are taught, that I may know how to sustain with a word him who is weary: he awakens morning by morning, he awakens my ear to hear as those who are taught.' (Isaiah 50:4)

253 (M)/1960.6.5/10.PR　　　　　　　8 September 1961

Daniel continues to impress us with his progress. His vocabulary has increased to the point where he can identify anything he wants or wishes to draw to our attention. He is even able to string together a sentence or two. For example, last week he said, in Hindustani, 'I eat potatoes and dal with roti. No yoghurt.' He has also developed a strong awareness of himself as an individual and as a member of our extended family here at CMCH. Daniel speaks of Pradeep as his 'dost' or friend and often gestures with one hand on his chest, repeating his own name and adding adjectives like 'good' or 'happy'.

We did have a disturbing incident, however, in August which

unsettled me more than it seems to have affected him. A visiting evangelist, from one of our supporting churches in Georgia, was touring India. His name is Reverend Floyd Corbin and he has a radio program called 'Heaven's Airwaves'. I had corresponded with him for several years but only met him for the first time during this visit. Floyd and his congregation at the New Light Gospel Church of Alpharetta, a suburb of Atlanta, have supported CMCH for almost a decade and we've been grateful for their generosity and prayers. At the same time, I have always had some reservations about their conservative and charismatic rhetoric. Though I am certainly not a proponent of liberal interpretations of scripture and believe in the fundamental truth of the crucifixion and resurrection, as well as the holy sacrament, I find phrases like, 'bathed in the blood of Christ', somewhat extreme. The hymn 'Are you Washed in the Blood of the Lamb?' has never been one that I appreciated, though it was a favourite of my mother's. In any case, when Floyd wrote to say that he would be in India, I invited him to visit us.

He arrived on a Wednesday and I asked him to preach a sermon the following Sunday. In the meantime, he had a chance to be a part of our community and see for himself the work that his ministry has supported. On the second day of his visit, he was introduced to Daniel and I told him something of the boy's story and the circumstances under which he came to us. I must have mentioned the superstitions and rumours that surrounded his arrival, particularly the idea that he might be a 'wolf-child'. Floyd was immediately intrigued and asked me a number of questions about Daniel.

'Has he learned to pray?' Floyd asked.

'Not yet,' I answered. 'He folds his hands in chapel but I'm not sure that he understands what it's all about.'

The look he gave me was something between disapproval and intense curiosity, the kind of expression that instinctively makes me nervous.

Nevertheless, I set my uncertainties aside and went about my work as usual, most of which involves accounts and administrative duties. None of it seems to have much to do directly with the Lord's Calling though it keeps CMCH running from day to day. A little later in the morning, when I emerged from my office, I could see Floyd sitting on the chabutra, a brick and concrete platform, beneath the peepul tree on the other side of the chapel. Daniel was with him, squatting on the ground, playing with a broken umbrella that he had industriously taken apart. I wondered whether I should go and speak to them but left it and went across to the boy's dormitory instead, where we'd called a plumber to repair one of the commodes.

On the way back to my office, I saw that Floyd had laid both hands on Daniel's head and was praying intently. Again, I didn't intervene.

Later in the evening, after dinner, Floyd went directly back to his room. He was staying in the guest suite at the back of my bungalow, which has a separate entrance. I had a stack of bills to deal with and he said that he was tired and ready to turn in early. About an hour later the lights went off, as they often do in Shakkarganj. Our power supply is erratic and the transformer near the village has a way of burning out at least once a month. As usual, I got my torch and went to light the petromax lantern that is kept in the dining room for these occasions. It was a quiet night, though I could hear a couple of dogs barking in the distance, as well as the shrill cheeping of bats and frogs croaking in the well.

Suddenly, I heard the scream of a child, coming from somewhere behind my house. By this time, everyone should have been inside the dormitory and I went out straight away with my torch, when I saw Daniel running across the compound in the dark. I chased after him as he rushed into one of the unlocked godowns, where we store garden equipment. When I entered, he was hiding behind several sacks of wood shavings that we use as mulch. In the glare of the torchlight, I could see that he was terrified and weeping. Not wanting to blind him with the light, I turned the torch beam aside and stooped down next to him. At the sound of my voice, his fear seemed to ease a little, though his whole body was trembling. When I took him in my arms, he began to resist and then clung to me, fiercely. I spoke in Hindustani, as reassuringly as I could and carried him back to the dorm. One of the aides has his quarters next door and I asked him to sit with Daniel until he fell asleep. By this time, he had quieted down, though he was still whimpering softly.

When I went back to the bungalow, Floyd was standing outside. Before I could even ask him what had happened he blurted out, 'That boy is possessed. He has the devil in him, that's for sure.'

'What do you mean?' I said.

'I was praying over him and Satan took hold of him and shook him like a broomstick. The boy began to abuse and curse me, even as I carried on praying.'

There was a strange look in Floyd's eyes, illuminated by the torchlight that cast a yellow pool around us. Sweating profusely, he mopped his face with a handkerchief.

'He must have just got scared when the lights went out,' I said.

'No, Elizabeth,' Floyd whispered. 'He's got the devil in him.'

Though I eventually went to bed, I was barely able to sleep and felt deeply disturbed by what had happened. For the next two days, I tried to keep Floyd away from Daniel. At one point, when I saw the boy sitting with Pradeep I went across and asked him how he was. He smiled and said, 'Okay,' though there was something distrustful in his gaze.

Then on Sunday, Floyd preached a sermon about the 'Wiles of Satan'. Of course, he spoke in English and I had to translate, which made me uncomfortable, as if he were putting words in my mouth. I have no doubt that there is evil in the world and the gospels make it clear that even Jesus was tempted by Satan. All of that, I am willing to believe, but Floyd spoke about the devil as if he were an evil spirit among us, like an illness or an epidemic, in the shape of a monster with fiery eyes and barbed claws. I tempered his descriptions and avoided translating much of what he said for fear of frightening the children but I could see the anxiety in their eyes, particularly when Floyd raised both arms and pretended to strike the devil with the sword of God.

After speaking for almost an hour, he had worked himself into a frenzy and stepped down from the pulpit into the aisle. The girls and women sit on one side and the men and boys on the other. It was a hot day and the fans were spinning overhead. Floyd began to advance towards Daniel and I knew what was coming. Just as I was about to intervene, Daniel let out a cry of alarm and rushed out of the chapel. Catching the evangelist by the shoulder, I held him back, letting the boy escape.

Fortunately, Floyd was scheduled to leave the next day and I was glad to be rid of him. Though I felt I should have confronted him and demanded to know what had taken place with Daniel, I knew he would never admit to the truth. Fortunately, the boy seemed to have escaped from any real harm. Over the next few days I made a point of observing him carefully, but he seemed unfazed by the incident. Though I thought of asking him what Floyd had done, I did not want to unsettle him with my questions or make him think it might have been his fault.

253 (M)/1960.6.5/11.PR   8 October 1961

Daniel is learning to play football and cricket. Though he still has some awkwardness to his movements, he is an athletic, energetic boy. He has been eating regularly with a balanced diet and I can see that his body is recovering from the deprivation and illness he had suffered from. The resilience of the physical body is so clearly linked to the healing of the mind. Often, I marvel at the complexity that God has created in each of us, our bones, muscles, sinews, veins, and each of the organs that keep us alive. Watching the children take part in sports, I believe it is as important as their classroom learning. I encourage them to get away from their blackboards and books and take part in physical activities.

Though we don't have a swimming pool, I take groups of

children to the canal nearby. Learning to swim is as important as lessons in multiplication or reading, for it can save your life. Yesterday, I took six boys to the canal, including Daniel. It was the first time I was introducing him to water and I wasn't sure how he would react. The place were we swim is just above the bridge, where the road crosses over and continues on to Amrudpur. There is a small barrage where the current turns back on itself. The water is only waist deep and perfectly safe. As a girl, I learned to swim here myself. After I had parked my jeep in the shade of a mango tree, the boys all jumped out and stripped down to their shorts. When Daniel saw the canal, I noticed a look of anticipation in his eyes and no apprehension or fear. Cautioning the boys not to wade out too far, I led them down the bank and stepped into the canal, gesturing for them to follow. Whenever I go swimming with the children, I wear an old cotton salwar kameez over my bathing suit to avoid embarrassment. Two of the boys already knew how to swim and I asked them to demonstrate for the others, kicking and splashing around in the cool, green waters. Daniel squatted on a spit of sand for a minute or two, following my instructions to wait, but when I beckoned to him, he eagerly sprang into the water, diving under and emerging ten or fifteen feet away from shore. Unlike the other boys, he swam with an effortless rhythm and his lithe brown body moved through the water like an otter. Before I could stop him, he swam out into the middle of the canal where it is much deeper, over his head. Surfacing, he waved to us and then reached the other side with a few easy strokes. I was completely dumbfounded and could not imagine how he had learned to swim. The other boys were impressed and looked at him with admiration, while only a few months ago they had made fun of him.

253 (M)/1960.6.5/12.PR 20 October 1961

This report is less about Daniel than it is about the incident that occurred in August with Floyd Corbin, the radio evangelist from Georgia. Ever since that night when I heard Daniel scream and found him cowering in the godown, I haven't known what to do. I have prayed about it so often but there seems no clear path to follow. Part of the problem is that I have no direct evidence that Floyd Corbin molested the boy, though from the circumstances, I am convinced he did. Daniel has said nothing to me, though he still struggles to communicate beyond the basics of language. The aides and ayahs haven't brought it up either. I know for sure the boy is not possessed by demons, but is simply a traumatized child, who needs our compassion and prayers, not the sound and fury of exorcism.

But this morning, I received a confidential letter from George Jenson, a missionary colleague who runs a village school near Raipur in Madhya Pradesh. Floyd Corbin visited their mission compound a couple of weeks after he was here in Shakkarganj. It seems they had a similar incident and George has reported him to the Overseas Mission Board, who were sponsoring his tour. In this case, the evangelist was found with a student in his bedroom and there was no doubt regarding his actions or motives. As George confessed, he did not report the incident to the local police because it might have been used against the school and it would, very likely, have been shut down. But he wanted to ask, if I had noticed anything unusual about Corbin's behaviour. Of course, I wrote back immediately and described what had happened with Daniel, telling George that he could quote me, when he submitted a report on the matter.

The vile depravity of someone like Floyd Corbin, preying on innocent children and then accusing them of being possessed by demons, is almost enough to shake the foundations of my faith. He is the kind of evil hypocrite that makes me understand that the devil exists in all of us. And I admit that I have been as guilty as him, because of my silence, failing to protect Daniel from this predator.

253 (M)/1960.6.5/13.PR 23 November 1961

As I was finishing breakfast this morning, I heard shouts of excitement outdoors and when I stepped onto the verandah, I could see a group of children had gathered by the front gate. Beyond them, on the other side of the gate, stood an elephant. When I went across to investigate, I could see that a sadhu was standing next to the elephant, begging for alms. In one hand he held a chimta with tiny cymbals that he clapped together to make a chiming noise. We often have mendicants like this passing through. Most of them are frauds and hucksters, preying on people's superstitions. As I reached the gate, I saw Daniel clamber over and stand next to the huge animal, with his cheek pressed against its flank, as if he were listening to the elephant's heartbeat. The huge creature seemed gentle enough and unbothered by the boy's presence, reaching over with the end of its trunk and brushing his arm with an affectionate gesture that was almost human.

The sadhu kept chanting his demands for alms along with verses in praise of Shiva and other Hindu gods. When he saw me, he grew more animated, though I shook my head and told him we were Christians and didn't require his blessings. This seemed to annoy him and turning towards Daniel, he tried to shoo the boy off with his chimta. But instead of stepping away, Daniel immediately reached up and caught hold of the lower lobe of the elephant's ear, as well as a strap that hung down from the makeshift howdah on its back. I called out and warned him to be careful but the animal was unperturbed and let him scramble up onto her back. Within a few seconds, Daniel was perched on the elephant's neck, his feet wedged behind her ears.

By this time, the sadhu was irate and began to shout at the boy, using language that did not befit a holy man. A couple of the other children now squeezed through the gate and I could see they had sticks of sugar cane in their hands. As the sadhu continued ranting, the elephant calmly accepted these snacks.

Wrapping the sugar cane in its trunk it began to chew contentedly, juice dribbling out from the sides of its mouth. Meanwhile, Daniel was beaming as he sat on top, completely at ease, as if he'd ridden on elephants many times before, though, as far as I know, this was the first time he'd seen one since coming to CMCH. I quickly went and got my camera from the house to take a picture of him perched there, like a miniature maharajah on parade.

It took a lot of persuasion to get him to come down but eventually he slid off the animal's back. In the end, I was forced to give the sadhu ten rupees to pacify him and he went off with a grudging salute. Daniel seemed pleased to be the centre of attention and I could tell there was a natural bond between him and the elephant, as if they trusted each other completely, though they'd never met before. All day, I have been puzzling over what happened. More and more, I am convinced that even if he wasn't raised by creatures in the wild, he must have spent a good deal of time with animals. Perhaps his parents were part of a circus or maybe they were itinerant herdsmen. Whatever it is, there is no question that he feels as comfortable with other species as he does with his own kind. In Genesis, it is written that God created man in his own image and gave him 'dominion over the fish of the sea and the birds of the air and over every living thing that moves upon the earth.' (Genesis 1: 28) And yet, in Daniel, I see a human child who lives in communion with other creatures rather than establishing dominion over lesser beasts.

253 (M)/1960.6.5/14.PR   25 December 1964

Christmas is always a joyous occasion at CMCH and it begins on Christmas Eve with carol singing, followed the next morning by a special service in the chapel and gifts distributed under a tree in my living room. We have sixty-two children at present and there is always happy chaos and confusion as they crowd into the house, with some spilling out onto the verandah. Ezekiel Masih dresses up as Father Christmas and hands out a gift to each child. This year we gave them all sweaters and woollen hats, for winter gets cold in Shakkarganj. We also handed out bags of sweets. Of course, the children get their uniforms and shoes at other times of the year but we like to celebrate the birth of Jesus with as much excitement as possible. We also have a feast of mutton pulao and other special dishes.

This morning, during the gift giving, I was surprised when I called out Daniel's name and he didn't come forward to receive his Christmas present. Looking around, I couldn't spot him in the crowd, so I set the gift aside and continued with the rest of the names. I assumed that he was somewhere at the back of the room or had been distracted by something else on the compound. His friend, Pradeep, sat in the front row and it was unusual to see him without his companion.

When the gifts had all been distributed and the children had dispersed to eat their sweets, I asked the aides if they'd seen Daniel around but everyone looked blank and I began to get concerned that he might have wandered off somewhere. Not wanting to disturb the celebrations and games, I went to look for him myself. He wasn't in the dormitory or in any of the usual places where the children congregate. I checked in the chapel and the dispensary but there was no sign of him.

The longer I searched, the more worried I became. Finally, I went around to the far side of the compound, where the ruins of the old sugar mill stand amidst a jungle of lantana and other weeds. The children are forbidden to come here for there are snakes in this area, including cobras. Often, I've thought of tearing down the ruins and clearing this area but I am reluctant because there is a lot of history in those old buildings. Besides, the weeds would grow back within a few months, even if we burned them to the ground.

I called Daniel's name a couple of times but got no reply as I skirted the ruins and entered the cemetery, which is enclosed by a fence. My parents and my brother are buried here, as well as a few former staff members and several children who have died in our care. Altogether, there may be twenty-five headstones. As I went inside and glanced around, I spotted Daniel crouched at the back, behind one of the graves. Though I called his name, he didn't look up but when I reached him, he was obviously distraught and had been crying. Lifting him into my arms I held him and asked what was troubling him. At first, he didn't respond and simply sobbed with the kind of emotions I hadn't seen in him before. He doesn't usually express his feelings the way the other children do and before this, I had only seen him cry once or twice.

Finally, when I got him to calm down, I asked what was wrong. In Hindustani he said that some of the older boys—he wouldn't reveal their names—had been teasing him and calling him a dirty monkey. They had told him that he wouldn't get any gifts for Christmas because he hadn't learned how to sing the carols or pray to Jesus on his birthday. All of this came out in a garbled rush of words and anguished sounds. Worst of all, he said they had called him a sinful animal for what he'd done with Reverend Floyd. Here he made an obscene gesture with his fingers, which the older boys had obviously used to taunt him.

Holding Daniel, weeping in my arms, I tried to reassure him but found myself in tears as well and at a loss for words, pained that he should face such ugliness and spite. Right then and there, I decided I would adopt him as my son. Over the years, I have cared for hundreds of children. Though I try to treat them with an equal measure of love and sympathy, I have never allowed a bond to form that goes beyond my duties as principal of CMCH. Yet, with Daniel, it is different and at that moment in the cemetery, as he sobbed in my arms, I wanted to run away with him and give him a new life, free from all the suffering and uncertainty that he has faced until now.

TWO

My earliest memories are suppressed beneath the stories I was later told, as well as my own retelling of those events. In this way, most of my childhood recollections have been painted over, like multiple coats of varnish covering the old doors and window frames of the bungalow in Shakkarganj, brushed on so thickly that the underlying grain and texture of the wood itself has been obscured. Yet, there are still a few moments that I can recall with perfect clarity, such as a wintry afternoon—which I later calculated must have been during January 1964—when Miss Cranston explained that she had adopted me as her son.

We were in the 'dufter', as she called it, a large study at the back of the bungalow, where the Miss Sahib had her desk and filing cabinets. The walls were lined with bookcases full of hardbound volumes as well as paperbacks, neatly arranged according to author and subject. Miss Cranston had labelled each of the shelves in her whiskery handwriting. A strong, medicinal odour permeated the dufter for the books were dusted with insecticide to protect them from silverfish and worms. Nobody was allowed to touch them, except for Miss Cranston, who would always lock the cases after choosing something to read.

On that particular day, we had just finished my English tutorial. By now, I had been at the Calvary Mission Children's Home for three-and-a-half years. Every afternoon, following tea, the Miss Sahib coached me in English. I had already learned Hindustani and could follow simple mathematics and some of the other subjects taught by Master Ezekiel Masih, and his assistant, Totli Babu, who spoke with a lisping stammer. All the children had an hour of English every day taught by the Miss Sahib but she insisted that I have an extra, individual lesson to help me catch up. Though I couldn't fully understand why, she had always favoured me over the rest of the children, which pleased but also worried me because it made others jealous and I was bullied when none of the adults were around.

Each time I came to the bungalow for my English tutorial, Miss Cranston would give me a toffee, or a piece of hard candy wrapped in bright coloured foil. In front of the others, she called me 'Daniel', but whenever we were alone it was always 'Mowgli'. I had no idea what this name meant or where it came from but it was a secret between us. Many of the other children had pet names like 'Guddu' or 'Tinky', so it didn't seem strange, though I never told anyone about it.

On the day that I learned of my adoption, Miss Cranston had read me a story from one of her books, then asked me what I had understood and if I had any questions. I don't remember which story it was but afterwards she took me into the dufter and sat me down in front of her typewriter, showing me the letters of the alphabet on the black and white keys. It was a large, upright Remington, a dusty green colour, trimmed with chrome and steel. Though I knew my ABCs, the letters on the typewriter were all mixed up. Leaning over me, Miss Cranston took a blank sheet of paper and rolled it into place. The typewriter made clicking sounds and had so many levers and buttons, I was afraid to touch it. But the Miss Sahib showed me how to press the keys and make the tiny metal arms reach up and tap the page. It seemed as if this mechanical creature was alive and I half expected the typewriter to crawl away on its own across the desk.

'Now, Mowgli, watch this,' the Miss Sahib said, placing her long white fingers on the keys the way Mr Samuel played the harmonium during chapel. As I sat there, she suddenly moved her fingers, quickly and firmly while the stem-like arms of the typewriter rattled. The scroll of paper began to move from right to left, as words appeared on its blank surface.

'Can you read what I've typed?'

I leaned forward and peered at the letters—D A N I E L. My name was followed by several other words I couldn't make out.

'It says, "Daniel is a smart boy",' the Miss Sahib explained.

After sliding the carriage return lever to one side, she took my hand in hers. Placing my index finger on one of the keys, she pressed it down hard so that the arm snapped up. After that, the Miss Sahib moved my finger, touching different keys, and typing five more letters.

'Now, see what you've written!' she exclaimed with a smile.

'Em Oh Dublu Gee El Aye.' I read out each of the letters but didn't know what sound they made together. Stepping back and looking at me with approval, the Miss Sahib pronounced my secret name, 'Mowgli!'

Miss Cranston then switched to Hindustani. 'There's something important that I've been wanting to tell you for a long time but I've waited until everything has been finalized. Are you listening?'

Looking up, I nodded expectantly.

'I haven't got a family,' she said. 'My parents are no more. My only brother died when he was fourteen. I never married because I was too busy with my work here at CMCH but I've always wanted to have a son like you.' Something in her tone of voice made me nervous, as she continued, hesitating between each word. 'Two years ago, I made a decision, Mowgli, that I would adopt you as my child. Do you know what that means?'

Though she continued to speak in Hindustani, she used the English word 'adopt'. I looked away, feeling self-conscious and uneasy. After a pause, she continued, picking up a thick file of papers on her desk.

'Yesterday, I received all the documents and permissions from the courts approving your adoption. Officially, you are now my son,' she said, flipping through the papers in the file. 'And I am your mother.'

Her voice had softened. I didn't know what to say. She had never spoken to me about this before. Nobody had asked me if I wanted to become Miss Cranston's son. It was like hearing words that no longer fit together and made no sense, just sounds—the way it was when I first arrived at CMCH. Yet, somehow, I understood that my life was about to change all over again.

'What about the others?' I asked, still staring at the typewriter.

'Who?' she said.

'The other children...here.'

'It doesn't matter,' Miss Cranston said, as if she hadn't understood my question. 'This is only about the two of us.'

I took a deep breath but no more words came out.

'Are you happy?' she asked me again.

I nodded, trying to smile, though I felt a hollowness inside my chest. The Miss Sahib wrapped both arms about me and held me tight, kissing me on the forehead. I was glad that nobody else was in the room.

When she finally let go and stepped back, I started to ask, 'Will everyone know?' but I said it so softly, she didn't hear.

She pointed to the typewriter again. 'Can you write your whole name?'

I stared at the keyboard as she rolled the paper up another line. Then Miss Cranston began to spell it out, 'Where's "D"?'

Finding the letter, I pushed the key so hard the tip of my finger hurt. Placing both hands on my shoulders, she prompted me, while I did the typing.

DANIEL CRANSTON

As if by magic, my new name appeared in black and white. It seemed as if nothing more needed to be said. I was her son. She was my mother. That was it.

In the evening, Shanti Ayah helped me move from the dormitory into Miss Cranston's bungalow. A room had been set up for me next to hers, with a charpoy on which we spread my mattress, sheets, and quilt. After Miss Cranston kissed me goodnight and switched off the overhead bulb, I lay awake for several hours, afraid of being on my own and worried what the other children might say. The old house had always seemed haunted, with its high ceilings and shadowy brick walls. This had been the planter's bungalow, when the compound was a sugar mill, long before it became an orphanage.

More than anything, it was the animal trophies that unsettled me. The Miss Sahib's father, Reverend Cranston, had been a hunter and many of the creatures he had killed were stuffed and mounted on the walls. Even in my room there were antlers of barasingha deer, with their skulls attached to wooden plaques. A leopard skin was draped across a table, its head facing my charpoy. The yellow glass eyes and yawning teeth were terrifying, even though I couldn't see them in the dark.

Most of the trophies were displayed in the living and dining rooms, including a tiger skin and the heads of sambar, chital, and hog deer, as well as a bearskin on the floor, which I always stepped around for fear it might spring to life. Two elephant tusks hung above the fireplace like an ivory arch. Earlier, whenever I had visited the bungalow, before my adoption, these creatures fascinated me but now that I was living among them, their presence was strangely disturbing, in ways I couldn't understand. As I went from room to room in the bungalow, the animals seemed to be watching me the whole time.

Many of the stuffed creatures were falling apart. A deer's nose had fallen off; a blackbuck had lost one of its spiral horns and the leopard was shedding its fur in patches that looked like mange. The bearskin had an unpleasant, musty odour, especially in the monsoon. One ear on a chital was missing and there were cobwebs between its antlers. Miss Cranston ignored the dead animals around her though sometimes she would tell me stories about her father pursuing the tiger through the forest after it had been wounded and became a man-eater. It had killed two men before Cranston Sahib tracked it down and shot the tiger in the heart.

After moving into the bungalow, I felt separated from the other children, though I still attended classes with them and spent most of the day in their company. Until then, I had struggled to fit in but now I was isolated again. Often, I could hear them snickering behind my back and calling me 'Jungli sahib' or 'Angrez ka baccha', son of a white person, and other names much crueller than that. They had always resented the special attention I got but now it was worse jealousy.

Even my best friend, Pradeep, began to treat me with resentment. Sometimes, when I tried to play with him, he would cock his head and laugh, 'Arrey, Daniel! Go back to your bungalow and forget about me.'

The truth is that I didn't have many more privileges than before. The food we ate was the same as they served in the dining hall, though Miss Cranston had gooseberry jam and guava jelly to put on our chapattis at breakfast and the bearers always served us first, bringing our meal across from the kitchen in an insulated tiffin carrier. She and I would sit side by side at the table and I was conscious of trying to eat politely instead of shovelling food into my mouth with my fingers. In the dining hall everyone ate with their hands or occasionally a spoon but in the bungalow the table was set with a fork, a spoon, and a knife, which the Miss Sahib taught me how to use.

She would do most of the talking at the table but if she asked me questions, I answered her as best as I could, learning not to speak when my mouth was full. Aside from everything else, the part I liked most of all was when Miss Cranston read stories to me in the evening, after dinner. Geckos would be chuckling on the wire mesh screens, hunting for mosquitoes. We sat together on the sofa in the living room and the lights often flickered because of the erratic power supply. Whenever the electricity went off, Miss Cranston would get up and light a petromax lantern, which hissed and gave off a chalky glow like moonlight.

She would read to me from books that she'd had since she was a girl, the Nancy Drew series and Enid Blyton, as well as stories about America like *The Adventures of Huckleberry Finn* and *The Adventures of Tom Sawyer*. Most of it I didn't understand but she would stop and explain some parts, so I could decipher enough of what was going on to be able to figure things out in my head. Just the sound of her voice gave me a comforting sense of being protected and safe, despite the animals staring down at me from the walls with their dusty glass eyes.

Three or four months after my adoption, I finally discovered why she called me Mowgli. The Miss Sahib began to read Kipling's stories to me. I loved the one about the mongoose, Rikki-Tikki-Tavi, who was the pet of a boy who lived in a bungalow like ours. Unlike the other stories, the names and places were familiar—Darzi, the tailorbird and Nag, the cobra. We also read *Just So Stories*—'How the Leopard Got its Spots' and 'How the Rhinoceros Got its Skin'. She told me that these were stories her father and mother had read to her when she was a girl of my age. I couldn't picture the Miss Sahib as a child for she was so tall and her face had a lean, stern look, except when she spoke to me. Around this time, she showed me photographs of herself as a child, standing on the verandah of the bungalow, which hadn't changed at all, and playing on the swing set, which was still there, near the girl's dormitory. In another photograph, she and her brother were posing beside the leopard her father had shot. There were also a number of snapshots of her with pet animals, including a barking deer that was feeding from her hand, as well as a baby porcupine that had been rescued from the scrub jungle behind the compound. In another picture, a palm squirrel sat on her shoulder while a parakeet was perched on her finger. As a child, she seemed to have raised a whole menagerie of animals adopted from the wild.

There were photographs of her parents too. Reverend and Mrs Cranston looked like something out of a history book, with their fussy clothes and pith helmets. There were pictures of the Miss Sahib, playing with some of the orphans from the children's home, riding a tricycle or holding a badminton racquet. Under some of the pictures in the album, which had thick black pages, her mother had written her name in white ink: 'Elizabeth Age 8'. When I pointed to this, she smiled. 'Nobody ever called me that, when I was a girl,' she said. 'I was always "Lizzie" or "Little Lizard", which was my father's name for me.'

I think she had been wanting to read *The Jungle Book* to me for some time but wasn't sure how I would react. One of the bookcases contained a whole set of *The Complete Works of Rudyard Kipling*, with rusty-red covers embossed in a flowing gold pattern of flowers, each of the titles at the top of the spine. I remember looking at them and wondering how anyone could write so many words.

'There's a boy named Mowgli in this book,' the Miss Sahib said, then added, 'But he's not you.'

The way she said it was awkward, as if Miss Cranston felt I might not like the story, or would find it strange that the boy shared my name. Then she opened the cream-coloured pages and began with a poem entitled, 'Night-Song in the Jungle':

> Now Rann, the Kite, brings home the night
> > That Mang, the Bat, sets free—
> The herds are shut in byre and hut,
> > For loosed till dawn are we.
> This is the hour of pride and power,
> > Talon and tush and claw.
> Oh, hear the call!—Good hunting all
> > That keep the Jungle Law.

Hearing the sound and rhythm of the words in her voice, I glanced up at the trophies on the walls. They seemed to be listening too. Then she started the story itself with the first chapter titled, 'Mowgli's Brothers':

> It was seven o'clock of a very warm evening in the Seeonee hills when Father Wolf woke up from his day's rest, scratched himself, yawned and spread out his paws one after the other to get rid of the sleepy feeling in the tips....

'What's a wolf?' I asked, for this was a word I hadn't heard before, though I guessed it was some kind of animal.

'A bhediya,' said the Miss Sahib. 'Do you know what that is?'

I shook my head.

'It's like a big wild dog,' she explained.

'Like a lakkad bagga?' I asked.

'That's a hyena, but yes, it's a little like that.'

She continued reading and I could follow most of the story though the language was complicated and the sentences seemed either too long or too short. I kept expecting Mowgli to appear. Finally, coming upon a child in the forest, Father Wolf cried, 'Man! A man cub. Look!'

Miss Cranston made each of the animals sound different, lowering her voice to a solemn growl when Father Wolf spoke and softening her tone when Mother Wolf replied. She snarled menacingly when Shere Khan, the tiger, demanded that the wolves hand over the man cub for his dinner. Her imitation of his rumbling voice made me lean closer and hold my breath. Eventually, we came to the part where the boy was given a name by Mother Wolf:

'O thou Mowgli—for Mowgli, the Frog, I will call thee,—the time will come when thou wilt hunt Shere Khan as he has hunted thee!'

The language in the book reminded me of Bible verses from chapel, with words like 'thee' and 'thou', which I'd only heard during worship services.

'Is Mowgli a frog or a man?' I asked.

'It's just a pet name Mother Wolf gives him,' said Miss Cranston.

'But a frog is "maindak" not "mowgli",' I insisted. In the well behind the kitchen there were plenty of frogs and the sound of their croaking echoed up from the dark, watery depths.

'Well, maybe the writer is just making it up. They do that sort of thing,' said Miss Cranston, before she carried on reading about Mowgli and the pack, and the lone wolf, Akela, who sat on Council Rock. Though most of the time, the Miss Sahib had a practical, no-nonsense manner, whenever she read a story to me, it was as if another part of her took over, a more whimsical, imaginative aspect of her personality, with an almost childish sense of wonder.

Now, as an adult, thinking back on that story and reading it again, there are many things that don't make sense. The book has a stilted, unconvincing narration and structure, while the whole idea of the wolf pack and the 'law of the jungle' seems contrived. Kipling makes it sound as if the animals are governed by rules laid down by a colonial magistrate and the sense of wild justice and fair play makes it confusing and difficult to understand their motives.

But as I child, hearing Miss Cranston read those words and give each animal a different voice, there was a mysterious yet convincing quality to the book that held my attention, though I never imagined this story could be mine.

THREE

The Miss Sahib stood six feet two inches tall with a slender but athletic physique. All the men and women who worked at CMCH were much shorter than her and she towered over us like the eucalyptus trees near the main gate. Her arms were strong but lean and when she picked me up it seemed to take no effort at all. The fingers on her hands were so long and supple, they seemed too large for her wrists. When she drove her jeep, I would watch the way she gripped the steering wheel and shifted gears, knowing that Miss Cranston was always in complete control. At the same time, when she was typing at her desk there was a graceful dexterity in her touch, as her fingers danced upon the keys.

She was an imposing woman, not just because of her height but also her features, which were white and smooth as porcelain, and almost as hard. The curved line of her jaw and chin, as well as the profile of her nose and forehead used to make me think of a teapot, not because of the shape, exactly, but on account of the moulded symmetry of its contours and the pale opacity of her complexion. Her eyes were a striking shade of blue, almost turquoise, and when she held me in her gaze it was impossible to look away. The colour of her hair was dusty blonde and she kept it braided in a single plait that reached to her waist. From the first time I saw her, I always thought she was beautiful but not in a conventional way, more like something out of nature, like a tall, graceful tree or a bird like a heron.

When she adopted me, the Miss Sahib would have been thirty-eight, still youthful but with a maturity that made me think she was already old. The clothes she wore were practical, usually a plain cotton dress of muted colours, belted at the waist and reaching just below her knees, with buttons down the front, a breast pocket and pointed collars like a man's shirt. Sometimes, she would wear salwar kameez or a cotton sari with a simple, block-printed border. Her shoes were mostly sandals or canvas sneakers. She wore no jewellery and her wristwatch was an ordinary Timex with a steel strap.

Sometimes it seemed as if Miss Cranston could have run the children's home entirely on her own, without anyone's help. She was able to do everything from repairing a leaking faucet to changing a flat tyre on the jeep or delivering a sermon at Sunday service. In the kitchen, she often joined the cooks in preparing our meals, insisting that they cut the onions as finely as she did, telling them to use less oil or add salt and spices to the dal. Though she never raised her voice, the Miss Sahib was clearly in command and everyone obeyed her orders, from Master Ezekiel Masih and Mr Samuel, who had worked for her father and still called her 'Lizzie Miss Sahib,' to the youngest child who had just arrived on the compound. I'm sure many of the employees resented her manner, which could be brusque and humourless, especially when she was annoyed. She had no patience for anyone who was lazy or careless. In a quiet but disapproving voice, she scolded the aides if they broke something or told the ayahs to do the laundry again if she felt the children's clothes, drying on a line, weren't clean enough.

When it came to money, the Miss Sahib was meticulous about her accounts. All of CMCH's expenses were noted down in thick ledgers and the receipts were tucked away in the filing cabinets. Though we never went hungry at the children's home, there was always a frugal sense of austerity. Nothing was replaced or thrown away until it had been worn to shreds or damaged beyond repair. Even in the bungalow, we lived very simply and many cups and glasses were cracked or chipped while the tablecloths and bedspreads were darned or patched.

Our meals were simple, usually dal and a vegetable, mostly potatoes, with rice or rotis. The only time we ate meat was when the Miss Sahib shot a wild boar or a nilgai. These animals lived in the scrub jungle across the dry riverbed and raided the fields in Shakkarganj. Miss Cranston had inherited her father's guns and the villagers would come and plead with her to shoot the wild pigs and other animals that destroyed their crops. Nilgai are antelopes, also known as blue bull, because of the grey-blue colour of their coats. They are as large as a horse with horns like a cow, which is how they get their name. We would often see them crossing the dry riverbed or standing at the edge of the fields early in the morning.

A few weeks after I moved into the bungalow, a group of villagers came to speak with Miss Cranston, complaining that a herd of nilgai had been feeding in their channa fields. That evening, she took out her father's rifle and wiped it with an oily rag. It was a heavy weapon, a .375 Magnum, with a scope. The bullets were thicker than my fingers. Two of the aides accompanied her and I went too. It was a dark night, with no moon, and we had a couple of torches. One of the villagers led us along an irrigation ditch, then down a slope to where a level patch of ground had been cultivated beside the riverbed. When we reached the fields, the villager gestured, whispering that the nilgai were already there though I could see nothing. Miss Cranston worked the bolt on the rifle and it made a soft gnashing sound of metal rubbing against metal. Then one of the aides switched on his torch, and shone it across the field. The light wavered for a moment before picking up the eyes of three animals standing about fifty metres away. They raised their long necks and stared at us, still chewing on the fresh channa. In the torchlight, the antelope looked almost tame, like tonga horses.

As Miss Cranston aimed at the nilgai, she looked like a statue in her salwar kameez, with her hair plaited down her back. The report of the rifle was so loud I jumped, even though I had covered my ears. There was a flash from the muzzle and the burning smell of gunpowder. The recoil made Miss Cranston stagger back a step though she quickly regained her balance and loaded another shell into the chamber. One of the nilgai had toppled over and was kicking its legs in the air. The other two had run away. Though I'd known what was going to happen, it startled me to see the animal on the ground as we all ran across the channa fields. By the time we got to the nilgai, it was dead and I could see blood coming out of its nose and mouth and a bullet hole in its side. Suddenly, the ground began to tilt beneath my feet and I was falling, though I remember nothing after that, except the Miss Sahib holding me in her arms and saying something in a comforting voice. When my head cleared, I was able to stand and I walked back to the bungalow holding her hand, knowing that I had fainted but not sure how or why it happened.

The nilgai was butchered that night and the next day the cooks made a huge curry for all the children. Sitting at the dining table in the bungalow, I took a few bites but thinking of the dead animal in the torchlight, with blood trickling from its nostrils, I lost my appetite.

Though Miss Cranston occasionally shot wild animals to help the villagers protect their fields and provide the children's home with meat, she wasn't a trophy hunter like her father, and more of a conservationist at heart. Every winter she would book one of the forest rest houses in the Hathi Talao Wildlife Sanctuary, for five or six nights, and take a group of children on an 'outing', as she called it. While this was the forest in which I'd been found, I had no memory of the place and when I went with the Miss Sahib to Hathi Talao, it was like seeing the jungle for the first time. Instead of the stuffed creatures on the bungalow walls, we came upon herds of deer and wild elephants too, as we drove through the forest in her jeep.

Back then, Hathi Talao was not a national park and tiger reserve as it is today. Very few people visited the sanctuary because the rest houses were poorly maintained and this area of Rohilkhand had a reputation for dacoits, who would waylay travellers and kidnap children. We heard these stories from the aides and ayahs at CMCH, who warned us that if we didn't behave, the 'dakus' would come and get us. The forests of Hathi Talao stretched all the way up to the border with Nepal and when I was growing up it seemed a dangerous, untamed, lawless region. However, the Miss Sahib never seemed to be afraid of dacoits or wild animals and she enjoyed these trips into the forest even more than we did, telling us stories about rogue elephants and man-eating tigers until our eyes grew wide with fear, though as long as I was with Miss Cranston, I wasn't really afraid.

On my first visit to Hathi Talao, a month before Miss Cranston announced that she had adopted me, we stayed at a rest house called Jhumri, overlooking the river, which was little more than a shallow stream during winter. This time, there were only boys on the trip. One of the cooks came with us to prepare our meals and eight of us piled into the jeep for the two-hour drive from Shakkarganj. Miss Cranston had attached a trailer and six of the older boys rode in that along with the luggage, bouncing along the forest road, covered in dust. When we reached Jhumri, it was the middle of the day and hot, so we all went down to the river to swim. Pradeep was with us and I carried him on my back, as I usually did. We were all excited and having a good time, stripping down to our shorts and splashing about in a pool of clear water that came up to our waists.

Less than half an hour later, we heard a shrill whistle from Miss Cranston. Even on the compound, she used to get our attention by blowing through her thumb and forefinger. Turning around, we saw her standing on the high bank next to the rest house, waving urgently. I knew something was wrong but in the bright sunlight there didn't seem to be any danger. Then I heard one of the boys shout.

'Hathi!'

Looking upriver, we saw four elephants coming in our direction. They were moving slowly but less than a hundred metres away. We all scrambled out of the water, leaving our clothes behind. Pradeep stared at me in panic, as if he were afraid I might abandon him. Hoisting him onto my shoulders, I began to stumble over the round river rocks. The other boys were ahead of us, running towards the path that led to the rest house.

'Hurry, Daniel. Hurry!' Pradeep shouted.

Looking over my shoulder, I could see the elephants crossing the river, coming after us at a steady, lumbering pace. By the time we reached the foot of the high bank, I was gasping for breath. The path up to the rest house was mostly loose sand and my feet kept slipping so that I couldn't make much progress up the slope. When I looked back, one of the elephants had gained on us and was hardly fifty metres behind, flapping its ears and raising its trunk. Just then, I saw Miss Cranston racing down to help us. She grabbed Pradeep off my back and told me to run as fast as I could.

I didn't think we would make it, but somehow we clambered up over the edge of the embankment and sprinted to the rest house. Rushing inside, we bolted the door, then crouched near the window. The elephants approached the rest house cautiously, still flapping their ears. One of them went over to the jeep and sniffed about with its trunk, then nudged it with its forehead. I wished that Miss Cranston had brought her rifle but she had explained that nobody was allowed to carry firearms into the sanctuary.

After a few minutes, the elephants seemed to lose interest in us, though one of them, a male with tusks, came over to the verandah and irritably brushed against a pillar, leaving a crack from top to bottom. After that, they headed off into the forest and we didn't see them again.

In the afternoon, Miss Cranston let us look at birds and animals through her field glasses. It was hard to get the focus right but I remember being amazed how close the deer appeared, as if I could reach out and touch them. She seemed to know the names of all the creatures in the forest and could identify their calls. The lapwings, she explained, cried out, 'Did you do it? Did you do it?' and the common hawk cuckoo had a call that sounded like, 'Brain fever! Brain fever!' I used to think she must know how to speak to the birds and understand their language.

Miss Cranston also knew the names of plants and trees, which she taught us to recognize—peepul and banyan, sal and shisham. The species that fascinated me most of all was one she pointed out near the bungalow at Jhumri. She called it a 'strangler fig' and explained how it was a parasite that wrapped itself around the trunk and branches of other trees, sucking moisture and nourishment from its host. I remember the web-like shape of the strangler fig embracing the dry trunk and shrivelled branches of a dead tree, which it had killed. Its pale green leaves were paisley shaped like a peepul and its tendrils were like dozens of snakes all twisted and knotted together. I found the strangler fig both fascinating and terrifying at once and when I went to bed that night, I imagined its serpentine limbs creeping through the window and suffocating me in my sleep.

In the evenings, we sat around a campfire with the amber light from the burning logs flickering across our faces, as Miss Cranston read aloud to us from Jim Corbett's *Man-Eaters of Kumaon*. Listening to the stories of tigers prowling the forest in search of human prey and the cunning strategies of the white hunter who tracked them down, the darkness behind us seemed full of ferocious beasts and invisible threats. Facing the roaring flames, I imagined that the fire protected me from hidden tigers crouching just out of sight.

One of the places where the Miss Sahib took us in the sanctuary was a ruined temple next to a spring-fed pond in the middle of the forest. Before we went there, she told me that it was her 'favourite spot on earth'. We arrived at the temple in the late afternoon, towards the end of a long drive through the park, looking for wild animals. I wasn't impressed, having expected something larger and more dramatic. Instead there was a green pool of water surrounded by reeds and broken-down walls overgrown with vines and creepers. But as we sat in the jeep, listening for sounds from the forest, the sun dropped lower in the sky and a golden light spread over the trees, illuminating the shimmering surface of the pond and glistening off the water lilies. Just then, a peacock gave a mournful cry and appeared on a broken parapet, its long tail silhouetted against the sunset.

'You see what I mean,' said the Miss Sahib leaning towards me.

'What kind of temple is it?' I asked.

'The forest guards say it's dedicated to Ganesh, the elephant-headed god, though nobody worships here any more,' she replied. 'Who knows? It's been abandoned for years yet I can't help feeling a spiritual atmosphere to this place.'

'But aren't all Hindus going to Hell?' I insisted, remembering what Ezekiel Masih had told us in chapel.

She looked at me and smiled. 'I'm not convinced about that. Praying to an elephant isn't the worst thing someone can do. Surely, it's no cause for damnation. In fact, to be honest, I don't think I actually believe in Hell.'

A few months later, in March, when Miss Cranston took a group of girls to the sanctuary, she insisted that I go along once again. Even before we left, the boys began to tease me and I tried to get out of it but the Miss Sahib ignored my protests. She made me sit in the front seat of the jeep between her and Shanti Ayah, who came along to do the cooking. This time we were going to a rest house called Bada Jheel, next to a lake at the southern edge of the sanctuary. Miss Cranston said it was a good place to see swamp deer, as well as migratory water birds. When we arrived, the chowkidar opened up both sides of the bungalow and the girls were put in one room with Shanti Ayah, while Miss Cranston and I shared the other suite. The surroundings were different from Jhumri, which had mostly thick sal and teak forest, whereas here the jungle opened out into wetlands and scrub jungle with babool or acacia trees. These were draped with weaver bird nests, like huge straw stockings. I preferred the other part of the sanctuary and wished we had the river nearby to swim in, for Bada Jheel was full of weeds and too marshy along the shore for anyone to wade into the water.

The girls played their own games while I sat apart from them, watching flights of ducks and geese circling the wetlands. In the late afternoon, Miss Cranston took the girls and me on a drive through a section of the sanctuary to see wildlife. At first, we came across nothing but a few red junglefowl and a couple of wild boar but as the sun began to set, we reached a dry watercourse where the Miss Sahib stopped the jeep and switched off the engine. Holding one finger to her mouth, she told us to be quiet and listen. Bird calls came from all directions. Then we heard a sambar belling in the forest to our right. The alarm call was repeated half a dozen times and Miss Cranston held up her hand, warning us to be silent.

Moments later, a tiger emerged from the tall grass and crossed the watercourse directly in front of us. One of the girls whimpered and another suppressed a squeal of fear but all of us were transfixed by the sight of the huge cat, which glanced at the jeep from a distance of fifty metres without breaking its stride. I could feel my heart rattling in my chest and my mouth went dry. Unlike the faded tiger skin that hung in the living room at home, this animal seemed to glow in the last rays of sunlight streaming through the trees. It was beautiful and terrifying at the same time. The muscles beneath its striped hide rippled with each step. We watched the tiger for less than sixty seconds before it disappeared into the grass on our left, but time seemed to stretch indefinitely and even after it was gone, an indelible image of the tiger was etched on the mirror of my mind.

When I looked up at Miss Cranston, she was grinning at me with an expression of delight. As she turned the jeep around and drove back through the gathering shadows, the girls couldn't stop jabbering about the tiger and how scared they'd been. By the time we got back to the rest house, the chowkidar had lit a campfire outside and I went and sat beside it. Staring into the burning logs, I could see an image of the tiger in the flames. After dinner, Miss Cranston read a couple of chapters from one of Jim Corbett's man-eater stories and everyone huddled together around the fire. I was glad when we went inside and bolted the door, crawling under my quilt and covering my head completely.

Hours later, I woke up to the sound of men's voices outside the rest house. Someone was banging on the door of the chowkidar's quarters and beams of torchlight shone through the windowpanes. Miss Cranston got up immediately and put on her dressing gown and sandals, going to the window and peering outside. Two shadows appeared on the verandah and I could see men carrying guns. One of them pounded on our door with his fist, telling us to open up and come outside. Next door, I could hear the girls whispering among themselves and the sound of someone crying.

'Who is it?' the Miss Sahib demanded, in Hindustani. 'What do you want?'

The men outside began to laugh, then shook the door so the

latch and hinges rattled. I stayed in bed, holding my breath, terrified. I knew these men were much more dangerous than any tiger.

'Who are you?' Miss Cranston called out, leaning against the wall and squinting through the window at the shadows moving from one side of the verandah to the other. Someone was hammering on the door next to ours and I heard the girls scream.

Then I saw the Miss Sahib reach up and unbolt the door. She had a torch in her other hand and switched it on as she stepped outside. The men's voices sounded coarse and ugly. I had trouble understanding what they were saying as Miss Cranston spoke to them. Slipping out of bed, I crept over to the window from where I could see her standing in the torchlight surrounded by four or five armed men. I could tell these weren't forest guards and knew they must be dacoits.

Moments later, a lone figure appeared in the yard, stepping out of the shadows. Miss Cranston shone her light on him and I could just make out a moustache bristling above a sinister smile. He was wearing a khaki shirt and trousers that looked like a uniform. In the torchlight, I could see that his long hair fell to his shoulders. Reaching into the pocket of his shirt, he took out a packet of cigarettes and lit one before he spoke.

'Lizzie Miss Sahib,' he said. 'Why are you here in the jungle alone?'

'I'm not alone. I've got twelve children with me,' Miss Cranston replied.

The man took a step forward, shielding his face from the glare of the torch, as the smoke from his cigarette spiralled up through the yellow beam of light.

'Don't worry, we won't hurt anyone,' he said. 'I didn't know it was you.'

Miss Cranston lowered the torch and I heard her speak his name for the first time, calling him 'Joseph'. They spoke in quiet, confidential tones, which made it impossible for me to hear what they said. A few minutes later, the man gestured for the others to leave and the rest of the dacoits disappeared into the night. After all the noise—fists pounding on doors and threatening voices–there was a strange calm to the scene. From her gestures, I could tell that Miss Cranston had known this man for a long time and they seemed to trust each other. He was shorter than the Miss Sahib by five or six inches, though he had a dangerous look about him, a rifle slung across one shoulder. The two of them spoke for a few minutes more and then he tossed his cigarette aside and slipped away into the forest shadows from where he'd come.

As a boy, the word 'dacoit' stirred up all kinds of fears and anxieties in me. Long before that night, when the dacoits came banging on the doors and Miss Cranston saved us, I had heard about the cruelty and ruthlessness of these criminal gangs. The staff at CMCH told us stories about the sadistic and bloodthirsty atrocities committed by dacoits. The victims were often children who were kidnapped, killed and chopped up into little pieces. Strangely, though, I hadn't heard of Yusuf Daku, until after the incident at Bada Jheel. When we got back to Shakkarganj and others learned of what had happened, suddenly there were plenty of stories to be told about this 'Isahi Daku' or 'Christian Dacoit', who had been raised at CMCH. It was as if his lore and legends had been suppressed out of a sense of shame and disapproval, but once people learned that Yusuf had spared our lives, he became a local hero within the Christian community.

For several days it was all we talked about. I learned that the Miss Sahib's parents had taken him in when he was a child of five, after his mother and father were arrested for robbery and murder. He came from a landless caste that the British designated as a 'criminal tribe', who were known for waylaying travellers along highways like the Grand Trunk Road. Growing up in CMCH, the little boy was christened 'Joseph' but later changed his name to 'Yusuf'. The year after he arrived in Shakkarganj, his parents were hanged in Bareilly Jail. We were told that he was the same age as Miss Cranston and Master Ezekiel Masih remembered that the two of them had been close childhood friends, growing up together on the compound. This was why Yusuf Daku had spared our lives, otherwise we would have been assaulted by his men and none of us would have lived to tell the tale.

When I asked the Miss Sahib if this was true, she smiled and shook her head.

'He was younger than me, a cute little boy. Some of the girls and I used to dress him up like a doll and play with him. When he grew older, he got into trouble a lot and finally my father had to expel him because he beat up another boy and threatened to cut his throat with a knife. We all felt sad that Joseph had to go because most of the time he was a fun-loving kid except when he lost his temper, then he just seemed to go mad.'

'How did you know it was him, that night, at the forest rest house?' I asked.

'I wasn't sure but a few days earlier I'd read an article in the newspaper reporting that he and his men were operating nearby. They had stopped a train on the narrow-gauge line up to Pilibhit, so I guessed it might be him. Of course, I hadn't seen Joseph for more than fifteen years.'

There were other stories about how Yusuf Daku had spared the lives of Christians though his gang had murdered dozens of people. The police had issued multiple warrants for his arrest but he hid out in the forests and scrub jungle along the Sarda River and often escaped into Nepal after committing a crime. Hearing these accounts, I kept remembering his dark silhouette standing in the torchlight with a cigarette tucked into one corner of his mouth. In my imagination, the dacoit was like a demon who hid amongst the dark layers of leaves, transforming himself into human form though he could just as easily change back into a treacherous spirit, haunting my dreams.

FOUR

Only a few of the orphans at CMCH were ever adopted. Most of them grew up in Shakkarganj, living in the Children's Home until the age of seventeen or eighteen, when they went off for higher education or to find a job. As the Miss Sahib explained to me, many years later, after we had moved to America, the legal process for adoption was difficult and unpredictable, especially for children that were taken abroad. At the same time very few people in India were willing to adopt orphans because of cultural and religious prejudices.

'A lot of it had to do with the caste system,' Miss Cranston told me. 'Most of the children we looked after at CMCH came from poor and disadvantaged communities. In many cases we didn't know anything about their parents but it was assumed that they were from low-caste, tribal or untouchable families. The stigma was very hard to overcome, even when they became adults and moved away from Shakkarganj.'

The only adoption that I can remember, other than my own, was of a young girl named Miriam, who came to CMCH as an infant, soon after I arrived. She suffered from some form of mental disability and I have clear memories of watching the ayahs looking after her. Though she was a bright-eyed girl with a cheerful smile, it took her four years before she could walk and a few of the crueller boys and girls would make fun of the way she moved her arms, with awkward, fidgety gestures. Among the children, and even some of the staff, there was an underlying prejudice towards those who had disabilities. It was natural, I suppose, because most of the children felt a sense of inferiority and by putting others down, they tried to elevate themselves. Early on, I was subjected to a lot of teasing and bullying too. It was one of the ways in which the children expressed their own anger, frustration, and loss. The Miss Sahib did her best to try and control this kind of behaviour and she would talk to us about compassion and love, but for those who felt dispossessed and abandoned themselves, it was difficult to care about the feelings of others.

Sometime around my fourth year in Shakkarganj, an American couple arrived for a visit. They were members of one of the supporting churches and, like most of the guests at CMCH, the couple stayed with Miss Cranston in her bungalow. I remember the man was very large, even taller than the Miss Sahib. He had light blonde hair and a pale complexion that flushed bright pink whenever he stepped out in the sun. His wife was a thin, dark-haired woman who wore red lipstick and matching nail varnish. Compared to Miss Cranston, who never used make-up, she looked as if everything about her had been painted on. The couple was very friendly and I remember shaking hands with the man, whose palm and fingers seemed four times as big as mine. Soon enough, rumours started to circulate that they were planning to adopt one of the children at CMCH. Among the boys in my dormitory, it became a joke and they would whisper about who might get chosen, teasing each other and pretending they didn't want to be the one.

Before the American couple left, we suddenly heard that they had picked Miriam. Everybody was shocked because she was the last child anyone expected to be adopted. The girl probably didn't understand most of what was going on and there was a lot of consternation and disbelief.

'Why her?' I remember overhearing the ayahs speaking. 'She's as dark as a crow and she'll never be able to finish school!'

'Why didn't they choose one of the baby boys? They're strong and healthy.'

'How will they look after her in America? The wretched girl needs someone helping her all the time.'

Miriam's paperwork took more than two years and by that time Miss Cranston had already adopted me. Amidst the confused emotions I felt was a sense of uncertainty about her motives. Had the Miss Sahib chosen me because, like Miriam, I was somehow disabled or less intelligent than the others? It made me vulnerable to the taunting of older boys and it also marked me as being privileged but also undeserving, as if my adoption were some kind of a reward for my inadequacies.

Soon after I moved into the bungalow with Miss Cranston, I remember asking her why the American couple had decided to adopt Miriam.

'Because they can't have any children of their own,' the Miss Sahib explained, which didn't answer my question.

'Will she get better in America?' I asked.

Miss Cranston tilted her head and looked at me across the table.

'Maybe,' she said, 'but I don't think Miriam will ever be able to live a completely normal life.'

I wanted to ask her more but the Miss Sahib changed the subject and began to speak to me about something else, switching from Hindustani to English. She always had a way of avoiding difficult questions and over the years I realized that it was impossible for me to argue with her because she held her opinions and beliefs deep inside where nobody could dispute or assail their integrity.

About six months after I was adopted, the Miss Sahib showed me my first passport, which was delivered by the postman who used to ride his bicycle up the canal road from Amrudpur. He was an elderly Muslim with a lace skullcap that matched his white beard. The khaki uniform he wore had brass buttons and the mailbag slung over his shoulder bulged with letters and parcels. My passport arrived during Ramzan and he cycled up to the bungalow looking exhausted. Miss Cranston offered him a glass of water but he waved it aside, saying that he was observing the fast. Because it was a registered letter, she had to sign for it and tipped him five rupees, which he accepted, raising his right hand in a weary salute before pedalling away to deliver other letters, telegrams, parcels, and money orders.

Tearing open the envelope, Miss Cranston took out the passport and flipped it open, glancing at my photograph and the information on the first page. She then handed it to me with a playful gesture, as if it were a riddle that I was supposed to solve. The cover was dark blue with the gilt emblem of an eagle stamped in the centre and the passport number perforated at the top. Inside, the blank pages were stiff and leathery with images of the American flag printed in pastel shades of red, white, and blue.

'What is it?' I asked, seeing the photograph of myself staring back at me.

'You're an American now,' said Miss Cranston. 'This is your passport from the US Embassy in Delhi.'

Holding it, I was confused. 'What's it for?'

'So you can travel with me to the United States some day,' she said.

'When?'

'Not for a while,' she replied. 'Maybe in a couple of years when I go back on furlough.'

'What's America like?' I asked.

Miss Cranston thought for a moment. 'It's different from here,' she said. 'More modern, with cars and highways....' She paused again, as if she wasn't quite sure what to say. 'They drive on the other side of the road.'

'Is everyone there like you?' I asked.

'No, Mowgli,' she said. 'No, there are black people and brown people too...all kinds of people.'

Looking down at my photograph with the crimped circular seal across one corner, I wondered if anyone in America really looked like me.

The Miss Sahib reached down and took the passport from my hand, saying, 'Here, let me put that in a safe place.'

I didn't tell any of my friends about becoming an American. Like my pet name, this was a secret between the Miss Sahib and me. Somehow, I still couldn't think of her as my mother and never have, which was a great disappointment for her. She wanted me to call her 'Mamma', because that was what she had called her mother. Though I tried a few times, it didn't sound right and I kept calling her 'Miss Sahib'. Eventually, she gave up, though she always introduced me as her son.

Fifty years later, studying my passport, which was recently renewed, I realize that virtually all the information it contains about me is false. The date of birth—6 May—is actually the day that I was brought to the Calvary Mission Children's Home. The year of birth is 1954, because Miss Cranston estimated that I was six or seven years old when I was found in 1960. She is listed as my only parent, for my real mother and father were never found, having disappeared into the void of India's anonymous millions. And where I came from remains a mystery. Though Shakkarganj is given as my place of birth, this is a bureaucratic charade created so that I could be issued this document that supposedly establishes my identity, even if none of it is true.

For half a century now, I've lived in America. As much as I can, I think of this country as home but there is still a sense of ambivalence sometimes, as if I don't completely belong. It's not just the look in other people's eyes or the questions I get asked: 'Where are you from...originally?' One gets used to that but there's something more beneath the surface, traces of a forgotten story, a personal history that's been erased. The human mind is a strange device...not just our brain but the thoughts and emotions it contains, recalling random images and sensations at odd times of the day or night, then switching off for no reason at all. What's forgotten can be as capricious as the things we remember.

I don't have a clear memory of many events from my childhood and much of what I recollect is fragmented like a broken mirror in which shards of the past are illuminated through fractured light. However, one of the things I do recall is the second visit of the American couple, when they came to take Miriam away. Thinking back on it, I realize that the Miss Sahib was able to help them complete the adoption, because she herself had recently been through the process with me.

They arrived in a car, driving all the way from Delhi, and stayed for a week with us in the bungalow. On the second day,

Miriam moved in with them and the couple began to take care of her themselves, with the help of the ayahs. By this time, she would have been six years old and more independent than before, though she still needed help eating and dressing herself, as well as with other daily routines. The first night, I heard Miriam crying loudly in the guest room on the other side of the bungalow and I knew she was unsettled and afraid. But the next morning, she sat happily with us at breakfast as one of the ayahs showed her new parents how to help her drink from a glass and feed her with a spoon. To begin with, the couple seemed awkward and unsure of themselves but soon enough they gained Miriam's trust and she let them comb and braid her hair and trim her fingernails.

From America, they had brought new clothes for Miriam and they dressed her up in these. Instead of her CMCH uniform, which was a pale blue salwar kameez, she now wore a yellow and white dress, patterned with flowers and a pink sweater. Miriam seemed delighted with the clothes but I could tell they made her uncomfortable. She hardly spoke, except for a few words that were difficult to understand. Later, they dressed her in leggings and a sweatshirt with new shoes that sparkled and she laughed when she looked at herself in a mirror.

The couple had also brought gifts for me, including a jacket with patch pockets in front that I put on and modelled for the Miss Sahib, then quickly took off before anyone else saw me wearing it. They also brought me a toy car, which ran on batteries and raced across the floor whenever it was switched on, colliding with the furniture and flipping over when it ran up against the tasselled edge of a durrie. I was so fascinated by this toy that I sat and stared at it for hours, as if entranced by the glossy red paint, studying every detail from the miniature tread on the tyres to the yellow stripes along each side and the headlights which flashed on and off like real lights on a car. When it was running, it made a humming sound like a wasp. Unlike the Miss Sahib's jeep, it had doors that opened and closed. Peering inside I could see the tiny steering wheel and plastic seats.

At the end of that week, when Miriam and her parents finally left, the whole compound turned out to see them off and she waved at us with her clumsy, fidgety hands. Miss Cranston kissed Miriam on her forehead through the open window of the car and then stepped back with a sad sort of smile on her face, her arms folded across her chest. The big car in which they'd come from Delhi drove off through the gate in a cloud of dust and when it settled they were out of sight.

Later in the day, holding the toy car in my hands, I wondered what it would be like to drive away from Shakkarganj and never come back, though I couldn't imagine it would ever happen to me. The Miss Sahib had explained that when they reached Delhi, Miriam and her parents would get into an airplane and they would fly all the way to America, on the other side of the world. It would take them a full three days before they got home.

The batteries in my car ran out after a couple of days and one of the headlights broke when it crashed into the leg of a dining chair. Miss Cranston warned me that batteries cost a lot of money but said she would buy me some more the next time she went to Amrudpur. Though the toy car wouldn't start any more, I pushed it along the floor and made a humming sound through my lips.

I didn't want to show it to the other children, except Pradeep, my best friend. Eventually, though, I carried it out of the bungalow and took the car across to the concrete chabutra under the peepul tree, where we often played. Pradeep asked if he could hold it and I made him promise not to break it, as I showed him all the different parts, including a spare tyre. Soon enough, however, a crowd of boys encircled us and one of them snatched my toy car out of Pradeep's hands and began to pass it around, turning it upside down and snapping the doors open and shut. I tried to make them stop and reached out to take it back, but they wouldn't give it to me. One of them set it down on the concrete and pushed it so hard that it fell on the ground and into the dust. Before I could pick it up, another boy had kicked it and soon there was a wild scrambling of feet as the boys booted the car about as if it were a football. Desperately, I threw myself into the middle to save my toy and got kicked in the ribs and stomach before I was able to run back to the bungalow with the car clutched to my chest.

Through my tears, I could see the damage. The car looked as if it had been in an accident. The front bumper and both headlights were smashed and one of the doors had broken off. The cover for the batteries had been cracked and hung loose, while one of the wheels was twisted at an angle. It was covered in dust and, even when I tried to wipe it off, the red paint seemed faded and old, the roof dented and scratched. I couldn't bear to look at my toy, it made me so sad, for I knew it would never work again, even if the Miss Sahib got me new batteries. At first, I thought I'd hide it somewhere in my room, but I knew that Miss Cranston would find it one day and ask me what had happened.

That evening, before dinner, when all the children had gone indoors, I carried my car, concealed under my shirt, and went across to the well, on the other side of the garden. We weren't supposed to go there because we might fall in and drown but nobody was watching as I approached the well. A circular brick parapet surrounded it and, reaching over, I threw my car in, hearing a splash moments later.

The next day, when Miss Cranston asked me about the toy, I told her that it was gone.

'What do you mean?' she said.

'I lost it,' I said.

'How?'

'I dropped it in the well by mistake,' I said, trying not to lie.

'Oh, Mowgli!' she said, with a disappointed sigh. 'How could you be so careless?'

But then, seeing that I had begun to weep, the Miss Sahib shook her head and took me in her arms, holding me while I sobbed, as if I were shedding a lifetime of tears all at once.

FIVE

The summer after Miriam was adopted and taken away to America, Miss Cranston and I were sitting at the dining table finishing supper. It was mid-May and oppressively hot, with no sign of the monsoon. A ceiling fan was spinning overhead though it barely seemed to churn the sultry air and I could see beads of sweat rolling down Miss Cranston's cheeks. Shambu Bearer, who brought our food, had left and we'd locked the door behind him. It was still early in the evening, a summer twilight, though the verandah lay in darkness. Suddenly, we heard a soft but insistent tapping. The sound seemed to be coming from the dufter door and grew more urgent. The Miss Sahib looked puzzled and pushed back her chair. My appetite had been robbed by the heat, so I also got up and followed her through, wondering who would come knocking at the back door.

When we switched on the light in the dufter, I could see a figure standing on the other side of the door but because of the glare off the windowpanes it took me a minute to realize who it was. By then, Miss Cranston had unlatched the door and helped Yusuf Daku enter. He was injured and limping badly from a gunshot wound in his thigh. I could see dark splashes of blood on the brick floor of the verandah and his trouser leg was soaked as well. When the Miss Sahib turned and saw me standing there, a look of uncertainty filled her eyes, as if she were about to tell me to go back and finish my dinner. But then she nodded.

'Daniel, go and get me some towels and a basin of water. Bring it to your room. We'll put him in there.' She spoke in Hindustani in a level, unemotional tone.

'The police ambushed us near the brick kilns on the outskirts of Amrudpur,' Yusuf said, swearing under his breath.

'Stop that, now,' the Miss Sahib warned him. 'I won't have you cursing in this house.'

The dacoit grimaced and fell silent.

By the time I'd found the towels and brought the basin, Miss Cranston had propped him up on my bed and she was already staunching the wound. The rifle he'd been carrying lay at the foot of the bed and there was a cartridge belt around his waist. A pistol was tucked into the belt, though he took it out and then removed the belt, setting them aside on the sheets.

'It's a good thing the bullet went all the way through and didn't hit a major artery,' Miss Cranston said. 'Still, you've lost a lot of blood.'

She had torn his trouser leg away and I could see the wound just above his knee. For a moment I thought I might faint, the way I did when Miss Cranston shot the nilgai. Some of the water sloshed from the basin onto the floor.

Yusuf winced as she wiped clotted blood away from the wound.

'Daniel, bring me some Dettol from the bathroom.'

I did as I was told, though my heart was beating frantically and I almost dropped the bottle as I took it down from the shelf.

'Most of my men were killed and the police must have captured the others,' Yusuf was saying, when I returned.

'How did you get here?' Miss Cranston asked.

'By motorcycle,' he said. 'It's parked outside the compound wall, behind the empty cowshed.'

'Did anyone see you coming in the gate?'

He shook his head then groaned as she disinfected the wound with Dettol. Again, I began to feel light-headed but the Miss Sahib beckoned to me.

'Another towel,' she said.

When I handed it to her, she wrapped it around his leg, tightly like a bandage.

'We'll stop the bleeding first,' she said. 'But you'll need to get to the hospital tomorrow morning, so they can take proper care of you.'

'No,' he said, his eyes fixed on my face. 'The police will be looking for me. I can't go to the hospital. Nobody should find out that I'm here.'

'How's that possible, Joseph?' Miss Cranston said, and for the first time I could hear anxiety in her voice. 'I can't hide you here forever?'

He looked at her with a pained expression.

'I have nowhere else to go,' he said. 'Lizzie Miss Sahib, you've got to help me until this heals.'

'A wound like that is sure to go septic. I can give you penicillin but I don't know if it will work,' she said, as if speaking to herself.

The dacoit stared in my direction, as if gazing right through me. 'Who's this?' he asked.

'Daniel,' the Miss Sahib answered. 'My son.'

He looked me over carefully, then spoke. 'Daniel. Bring me a glass of water.'

I ran to the dining room, where the remains of our dinner was still on the table. Picking up one of the water glasses, I filled it from the jug and carried it back, holding it with both hands because they were shaking.

When I came into the room, Miss Cranston was standing with one hand on Yusuf's head. At first, I thought she was praying but then I realized she was simply comforting him. He took the glass from me and drank the water slowly but steadily until it was finished, after which he set it aside and wiped his moustache with the back of his hand.

Reaching into his shirt pocket, he took out a packet of cigarettes and put one in his mouth, before checking to see if he had any matches. I could see a look of disapproval cross the Miss Sahib's face but she said nothing.

'Can I have a light?' Yusuf asked, 'My matches must have fallen out of my pocket.'

Miss Cranston walked across to the chest of drawers, where she kept a box next to a candlestick. She had a strict rule at CMCH that nobody was allowed to smoke inside the compound but she didn't stop Yusuf, as he lit up and inhaled deeply, then let the smoke stream out of his mouth as he spoke.

'How long has he been your son?' The dacoit kept staring at me, as if trying to figure out who I was.

'About three-and-a-half years,' Miss Cranston replied. She reached across and switched on the fan, for the room was suffocating. The cigarette smoke spun away into the corners like drifting cobwebs. After that, she went and got some pills from her medicine cabinet and gave him more water with which to swallow them. His breathing had eased a little and there was a spot of blood seeping through the towel, though it seemed to have mostly stopped. Yusuf's body was trembling, as if he were cold, despite the heat, and the Miss Sahib drew a sheet up to his shoulders.

'Daniel, you can sleep in my room tonight,' she said to me. 'But first help me clean up. Bring the bucket from my bathroom and the mop.'

By the time we had washed the blood off the verandah and floors it was almost midnight. Yusuf seemed to be asleep, though he opened his eyes when we checked on him and lit another cigarette.

Miss Cranston made up the divan at the foot of her bed for me and I was glad not to be sleeping alone that night, after all the blood I'd seen. Before we fell asleep, the Miss Sahib said to me, 'Mowgli, you can't tell anyone he's here. Do you understand?'

'Yes, I know,' I said.

In the morning, when I woke up, for a few seconds I thought it must have all been a bad dream but then I realized where I was. The first light of dawn filtered through the roshandan, or skylight, and it was still hot inside the bungalow, even with the fan whirling overhead.

The Miss Sahib was already awake and she had made her tea in the kitchen along with a cup for our guest. Through the open door, I could see that he was sitting up in my bed, just as we had left him. The stench of stale tobacco smoke filtered into the Miss Sahib's room. I could hear them talking quietly, but couldn't make out what they were saying.

Later on, Miss Cranston brought me a clean set of clothes and told me to wash up in her bathroom.

'Today, you'll stay indoors,' she said, 'and not go to class. I'll tell the teachers you're sick and we'll use that as an excuse to keep everyone away.'

Lying was one of the things Miss Cranston had always warned me about but I knew the situation was desperate.

'What about his motorcycle?' I asked. 'Won't the police find it?'

She glanced at me with a worried look, then said, 'I've asked Amos to park it in the angan, out of sight.'

'Does Amos know that Yusuf Daku is here?'

'His name is Joseph,' Miss Cranston corrected me. 'I had to tell someone. Amos will keep it to himself.'

'What happens if the police come looking for him?'

She stared at me with a lost expression.

'I don't know, Mowgli. I just don't know.'

For a moment, I thought she was going to break down and cry but she pulled herself together.

Shambu Bearer delivered our breakfast while I stayed in the bedroom and Miss Cranston brought us each a bowl of porridge, as well as parathas with jam. After that, she went across to see how the rest of the children were doing and to give them their English lesson. I was sitting in the Miss Sahib's bedroom when Yusuf called out.

'Daniel! I need your help.'

Stepping through the door, I saw that he was standing beside the bed with one hand braced against the wall. His long, lank hair fell over his face, though he brushed it back.

'I need to take a piss,' he said. 'Give me your shoulder.'

Going across to the other side of the bed, I let him lean his weight on me, as he hobbled into the bathroom. The pain must have been severe but in the end, he got to the toilet and relieved himself. I looked away, though I could hear the sound of his urine spattering against the porcelain. Below the torn pant leg, the wound looked as if it were drying up, though that part of his thigh was a dark, bruised colour. Once he got back to bed, Yusuf covered it with the towel again, sucking in each breath with an effort. He then pointed to his rifle.

'Bring that over here,' he said.

Lifting the weapon, I put it in his hands and watched as he worked the bolt, then added a couple of cartridges from his belt and filled the clip. After that he took his pistol and loaded it as well. Aiming at the leopard skin on the table facing the bed, he pretended to fire several times and then, pointed the pistol at one of the barasingha trophies on the wall.

'I killed a bigger deer than that a couple of weeks ago,' he said. 'There was so much meat we couldn't eat it all and half of it went bad because of the heat.'

'The Miss Sahib shot a nilgai last month,' I said.

He looked at me with a curious expression.

'What guns does she use?' he asked.

Realizing my mistake, I fell silent.

'Oi, Daniel. Does she still have her father's rifle and shotgun?' he demanded.

I nodded.

'Where are they kept?'

I said nothing but after a moment he laughed, then raised the pistol and pointed it at me.

'I asked you a question,' he said. 'Where does she keep her guns and ammunition?'

Tears began streaming from my eyes as I looked into the pistol's muzzle, wondering if I would be dead before I heard it go off.

'In her steel cupboard. In the dufter,' I heard myself say.

'Good boy,' he said, laughing again. 'I'm only teasing you. Don't worry. I won't shoot you but if I ask you for the guns, do you promise to bring them to me?'

I nodded as he lowered the pistol and then gestured for me to sit on the bed. The sweat was dribbling down my spine and I wanted to run out of the room but couldn't move my legs.

'Come here,' Yusuf said. 'I'm sorry, I scared you. Don't worry, I only shoot deer...and leopards, tigers, and elephants...and sometimes policemen.'

I looked at him and sat on the edge of the charpoy. He laughed again and lit a cigarette. I could see there was only one left in the packet.

'Tell me something,' he said. 'Why do you think the Miss Sahib chose you as her son? There are so many other boys and girls here. Why you?'

My mouth was almost too dry to speak. I glanced at him to see if he was still teasing me but there was a serious look in his eyes.

'I don't know,' I mumbled.

'Maybe she thought you were the loneliest child of all,' he said, then after a pause he added, 'like me.'

'Why were you lonely?' I asked.

He looked up at the ceiling for a moment, as if trying to think back.

'When I first came here to the Children's Home, I was so scared I couldn't sleep at night. My father and mother were in jail, arrested by the police. Later, they hanged them, one after the other, from the same gallows. My mother had to watch my father go first. When I heard what had happened to them, I felt even more afraid and alone, but also angry. I promised myself that I would kill every policeman responsible for their deaths.'

His tone of voice was something between a whisper and a curse.

'Lizzie Miss Sahib was the only one who understood,' he said. 'She was like an elder sister I never had. When I cried, she would hold me. Sometimes she would bring me into this house and let me play in her room. It was on the other side of the house, facing the chicken coops. Is that room still there?'

'It's a storeroom now,' I said.

'She was the only one who could make me laugh,' he said.

For a minute or two the dacoit was silent, drawing the smoke from his cigarette into his lungs and squinting, as he watched the shadow of the ceiling fan rotating on the wall.

'What happened to your parents?' he asked, abruptly.

It took me a moment to reply, 'I don't know.'

'Why?' he said. 'Did your mother just throw you away?'

There was cruelty in his question, the way the older boys taunted me sometimes.

'I was found in the jungle,' I said.

'Which jungle?' he demanded.

'Hathi Talao. Two forest guards found me and brought me here. They said I was raised by wild animals.'

He smiled and ran his tongue over his lips.

'Is it true?'

I shrugged. 'I don't remember.'

'Who says this?' he asked.

'Some of the other children. They say that I'm half-animal and call me names like bandar ka bachhaa, son of a monkey.'

He didn't laugh, as I had expected him to.

'What does the Miss Sahib say?' he asked.

'She calls me Mowgli,' I said.

'Mowgli? What's that?'

'It's a name from a book. It doesn't mean anything.'

The cigarette had burned down to a stub and he leaned over and crushed it on the brick floor.

'She used to read books to me also,' Yusuf said. 'I didn't understand most of the stories but she would point to the words and make me repeat them. I never learned English except a few bad words like "bloody fool".'

I tried to hide my smile but he saw it and laughed.

'Don't tell the Miss Sahib I used those words in front of you,' he warned me, placing one hand on the pistol that lay beside him.

'Have you always been a daku?' I asked.

His gaze narrowed.

'Who says I'm a daku?'

'The others,' I replied, afraid that he would lose his temper. His mood seemed to change every minute, sometimes calm and other times angry or suspicious.

He looked up at the roshandan, where a gecko was silhouetted against the dusty windowpane, then he moved his injured leg, grimacing with pain.

'Why did the police shoot you?' I asked.

'Because they had nothing better to do,' Yusuf replied, with a cynical wave of his hand.

Later, I learned that he and his men had attacked the home of a wealthy merchant in Amrudpur, from whom they were trying to extort money. When the man resisted, Yusuf and his gang shot him in the head and killed two of his sons. The dacoits then looted the house and took off in the direction of Pilibhit though the police had been alerted and set up a roadblock along the highway. Yusuf was driving a car he had stolen from the merchant's house. Four others were with him in the car and three of his gang members were on motorcycles. When they saw the roadblock, they tried to turn around but the car's tyres were shot out and it swerved into a ditch at the side of the highway. The police then closed in on the gang and the gun battle lasted half an hour. Five of the dacoits were killed and two captured, while Yusuf escaped on one of the motorcycles. Three policemen were shot dead in the encounter.

Miss Cranston must have read all this in the newspaper by the time she returned to the bungalow late in the morning. She asked me to go into the other room and then told Yusuf that he had to leave immediately because his presence threatened the safety of all the children and staff at CMCH. I was worried that he might lose his temper and shoot her with his gun, but neither of them raised their voices. The Miss Sahib spoke firmly but quietly, telling him that he had to take responsibility for his crimes and surrender to the police. I listened to as much as I could hear through a crack in the door.

'If I surrender, they will torture me,' he said, 'and in the end they'll kill me anyway. Better to take my chances.'

'But all your men are either dead or captured,' she said. 'And with that bullet hole in your leg there's nowhere you can go.'

'I can still ride the motorcycle,' he said. 'And there are people who owe me protection.'

'Then why did you come here?' Miss Cranston asked. 'Why didn't you go and get help from them to begin with?'

'This was the closest place I could hide. When I escaped the police, I came along the canal road. It brought me here.'

'You're endangering all of us,' said the Miss Sahib. 'You'll have to leave right away. I'm afraid I can't help you any more.'

There was silence for almost a minute, then I heard Yusuf speak. 'At least let me stay until it gets dark,' he pleaded. 'Then I'll take the motorcycle and go.'

Miss Cranston didn't reply but a few moments later she came out of the room and I knew she was upset, tears in her eyes. She went into the living room and sat down on the sofa, holding her head in her hands. I could see her shoulders shaking as she wept. As I watched from the bedroom door, the shadows of the hunting trophies hanging on the walls seemed to be staring down at her like the silent ghosts of creatures from a forgotten forest. Just then, the electricity went off and the fans came to a stop.

A little while later, I heard Yusuf call me.

'Oi Daniel! Come and help me go to the toilet.'

Turning slowly, I went across and pushed open the door. He was still sitting on the bed and waved for me to come around to his right side. This time, when he got to his feet, he put more weight on me and I thought he was going to fall as we staggered across to the bathroom. The whole time he was swearing under his breath because of the pain. After that, when I got him back to bed, he took the last cigarette from the packet and lit it, as if it were a fuse on a firecracker, his hand shaking badly.

'What's that name the Miss Sahib calls you?' he asked.

'Mowgli', I told him.

'Mughlai!' he joked. 'Murg Mughlai! I need your help.'

I looked at him without speaking.

'Can you get me more cigarettes?' he said.

'Nobody is allowed to smoke on the compound,' I replied.

He laughed. 'That means nothing, Mughlai. I'm sure you know where to find some tobacco. At your age, all of us were smoking.'

His eyes studied me through a veil of smoke. The electricity was still off and there was a stillness to the room, as if the air had congealed around us.

'What do you say? Are you going to help me or not?'

I tried to shake my head but there was no way to refuse him. Turning around, I passed through the Miss Sahib's bedroom and into the living room. She had gone by this time, locking the front door behind her. I tried to open it but could feel that the latch had been drawn from outside. Of course, there was another way out, through the dufter and onto the back verandah.

From there I crossed the yard with a strange feeling of being watched. It was midday and the sun was so hot it scorched my skin and made my eyes burn. Keeping to the shade as much as possible, I cut behind the dining hall and the boys' dormitory to the ruins of the old sugar mill. The smokestacks looked like the trunks of dead palm trees. Ducking under a thicket of lantana, I crawled over to the broken remains of a brick wall. One of the bricks was loose and I pulled it out, reaching in to find the two packets of bidis I'd hidden there. A boy named Aseem had traded them for a bar of chocolate that the Miss Sahib had given me. Though I'd tried a couple of bidis, the harsh smoke hurt my throat and I was worried that Miss Cranston might smell the tobacco on my breath.

Slipping back through the vegetable gardens and along the hedge leading to the bungalow, I returned within ten minutes, hiding the bundles of bidis in the pocket of my shorts. Latching the dufter door behind me, I crept into my room, where the dacoit still lay on the bed, his dried blood staining my sheets. Indoors it was slightly cooler than it was outside but stifling with the fans off. I could see that the wound in his leg was swollen and starting to ooze with pus.

'501,' Yusuf muttered, reading the label on the bidi bundle. 'Thank you, Mughlai bhai. Will you smoke one with me?'

He offered me a bidi and laughed when I shook my head.

'Don't pretend you don't smoke,' he said, as he put the bidi to his lips and brushed his moustache aside before lighting up. 'I won't tell her, I promise. This will be a secret between the two of us.'

'I've only tried once or twice,' I said. 'It made me cough.'

'You'll get used to it soon enough,' he said, then looked around the room. 'I don't suppose you could get any liquor for me.'

The look of alarm on my face made him laugh again. Miss Cranston was even more strict about alcohol. Only last month she had sacked Ishmael Mali, the gardener, for coming to work drunk.

Yusuf shook his head, 'I didn't think so,' he said. 'Though it would help ease the pain. This evening, when I get out of here, the first thing I'll do is get a bottle of Shahjahanpur rum.'

At that point the electricity came on and a bulb above the dressing table flickered, the filament glowing like Yusuf's bidi, giving off very little light. The fan overhead began to turn listlessly at first and then picked up speed until its blades disappeared into a shadowy blur. Yusuf Daku fell silent, closing his eyes. For a while it seemed as if he had fallen asleep, though I knew he would wake up at the slightest sound. I sat as still as I could feeling the air whirling around us.

Several hours later, Miss Cranston returned and gave Yusuf the key to his motorcycle.

'It's parked at the back in the angan,' she said, then sniffed the air. 'Your cigarettes were bad enough but the bidis smell worse.'

Yusuf looked at me and winked.

'Don't worry, Lizzie Miss Sahib, I'll be gone very soon and you'll never see me again.' Then he looked at me. 'He's a good boy, your son.'

'Yes, he is,' she said with a smile.

'Daniel told me he was found in the jungle,' Yusuf said.

'That's true,' Miss Cranston replied.

'Do you think he was raised by wild animals?' Yusuf gestured towards the leopard skin and the antlers on the wall.

'No, of course not,' she said.

'Then how did he survive? The jungle is a dangerous place,' said Yusuf. 'Even for someone like me, armed with a rifle. How could a helpless child stay alive for more than a day or two?'

Miss Cranston gave me an anxious look. 'We don't know, but God protected him and sent him to us.'

'God...' The dacoit said softly, flicking the burnt-out end of his bidi onto the floor. 'I suppose he does protect us, doesn't he?'

'You should pray to him, Joseph,' she said, 'and ask for forgiveness. The Lord will never betray you if you ask for his help.'

Yusuf's eyes were bloodshot and I could see that he was sweating.

'I don't pray that often,' he said.

'Remember, Jesus died for your sins,' Miss Cranston said, reaching over and putting her hand on my shoulder, as if she was talking to both of us. 'He knows your thoughts, your dreams, everything about you. There is nothing you can hide from him. Pray to him and he will relieve you of your suffering.'

After that, she lowered her head and remained silent for several minutes. Yusuf kept his eyes open. I could see that he wasn't praying, simply staring into the shadows in one corner of the room.

Finally, Miss Cranston took a deep breath and glanced at her watch.

'It's past four o'clock,' she said. 'I have to go and check the laundry. Today is dhobi day. By the time I come back, I hope you'll be gone.'

Yusuf put another bidi in his mouth but didn't light it. He spoke while holding it between his lips.

'Thank you,' he said. 'I'm grateful to you for not telling the police and for letting me stay here, at least for a night.'

'God protect you,' she said, putting out her hand, the long white fingers brushing his cheek. He did not move. 'Goodbye, Joseph.'

'Goodbye,' he said in English.

'Come with me, Daniel,' Miss Cranston said.

I hesitated and Yusuf smiled.

'Let him stay. What's he going to do, count laundry?' he said. 'I promise, I won't harm him and he can help me get onto the motorcycle. I'll need a hand.'

The Miss Sahib looked down at me, then checked her watch again and left the room. Yusuf lit his bidi and asked me to go and bring him some water. It looked as if he had a fever and I could see that he was sweating even more than before.

When I got back with the water, Yusuf eyed me with a strange look, as if he were having trouble focusing.

'Mughlai bhai,' he said. 'Do you believe in God?'
I nodded.
'Which one?' he asked.
'Yesu Masih,' I said.
He looked away, staring into the leopard's glass eyes.
'Yes, Yesu Masih must have protected you from this baghera. Look at his teeth, they could crush your neck and those claws would tear you apart. He would have eaten you up like a Mughlai chicken.'
I laughed, more out of nervousness than anything else.
Yusuf set aside the glass of water without taking a sip. Picking up his rifle, he aimed it at the leopard's head, making the sound of bullet by blowing through his teeth, 'Tchnyoow! Tchnyoow!'
Then he put the weapon down and drank the water.
'I want to tell you a story before I go,' he said, gesturing for me to take a seat on the edge of the charpoy.
'How old are you?' he asked.
'Thirteen,' I said.
He thought for a moment, then spoke. 'About eight or nine years ago, I can't remember exactly, my men and I were camped on the other side of the Sarda River, near the Nepal border. It's a miserable place, no paved roads, nothing but mosquitoes and flies. The villagers are poor and nobody cares for those people. There was a politician named Gaurav Thakur who was up for re-election. He was a corrupt man who had been representing that district for years. His men were bigger thugs than us but he got a lot of money from his party to win the election, boxes of cash that he distributed to all the headmen of the villages to buy their votes.

'I heard about it and thought, why shouldn't I get my share? So, one day, my men and I heard that he would be visiting a village near the place where we were staying. We waited for him as he came by with a police escort and another vehicle with a loudspeaker, praising his name.'

Yusuf drained the glass of water and blinked, while I wondered why he was telling me this story.

'When Gaurav Thakur stopped at the village to meet with the

voters, I sent one of my men, Singara, to speak with him. My message was simple. I would offer him support and, with my connections in the area, I could help influence the vote.

'After finishing at the village, he told Singara to get into his vehicle so that he could discuss things with him. Then they drove a short distance out into the fields and his men beat Singara up badly, telling him that they didn't want any help from criminals like me. He called me all sorts of names including "a low-caste Christian pariah", all of which Singara told me once we picked him up from the side of the road and took him to a doctor. Three of his ribs were broken and they'd knocked out most of his teeth.'

Yusuf paused for a moment and wiped the sweat from his forehead.

'I'm explaining all this, so you understand why we did what we did. Gaurav Thakur was a criminal and he had several murders to his name. Anyway, I decided to teach him a lesson. After asking around, we learned that his son was studying in Nainital. The boy was seven years old, named Anil. Soon, we shifted our base to a forested belt at the foot of the mountains between Haldwani and Tanakpur. It was a place where we'd camped before. I sent three of my men up to Nainital to locate the boy. He was studying in an expensive English-medium school..., I forget the name. My men paid off one of the sweepers who worked in the dormitory. He told them which of the students was Anil. The next day, after school let out, they waited until he was playing outside with his friends. When nobody was looking, my men kidnapped the boy and drugged him, then brought him down the hill.

'Knowing that the police would be searching for us, I decided that we should move out of the district before we contacted Gaurav Thakur and demanded a payment for his son's life. That same night we moved on to Hathi Talao, taking the boy with us.'

Yusuf was watching me as he told the story, trying to gauge my reaction. I was sitting on the bed, half-turned towards him. As I began to understand his purpose in telling me this story, I felt a clutch of fear in my throat, like someone's fingers closing on my windpipe. Yusuf's voice seemed to have slowed down and the words became slurred.

'We often camped in the sanctuary, upriver from Jhumri, a quiet, isolated place where the forest guards wouldn't bother us and there were plenty of wildfowl and deer for us to hunt. Until this point, I hadn't spoken to the kidnapped boy but in the evening my men brought him to my tent. He was still half-drugged but alert enough to be frightened. I asked his name. He said it was Anil, stammering with fear. I told him we wouldn't hurt him if he didn't try to run away. After that, I sent one of my gang members to the nearest town to telephone Gaurav Thakur. We demanded ten lakhs for the safety of his son.'

Yusuf stopped for a moment and turned his head, as if trying to remember exactly what had happened, though he also seemed to be listening to a sound from outside. For a few seconds he was distracted, then glanced back at me.

'It took two days for my man to go and come from Bareilly. Meanwhile, the boy was refusing to eat and at night he would cry and cry. We had a transistor radio and kept listening to the news to find out if there was any report on the kidnapping but in the forest the signal was weak and all we could get was Radio Najibabad, which played mostly music. After the second day, my men were complaining that the boy was driving them mad with his wailing and whining. They were keeping him in a bamboo hut we'd built and I had them bring him to me again. This time I said, "Anil, we've written to your father, Gaurav Thakur, and if he pays us the money we've demanded you'll go home safe."

'The boy looked at me in a strange sort of way that made me hesitate.

'"What's your father's name?" I asked. He spoke with a stammer but finally got it out, some other name completely. Later that evening, my man came back from the town. He had spoken to Gaurav Thakur, who told him that we had kidnapped the wrong child. His son was perfectly safe. My man had brought a newspaper in which there was a short article about the kidnapping, giving the boy's name as

Anil Kumar Shukla, or something like that. I can't remember exactly.

'After we discovered our mistake, my men suggested we kill the boy and get rid of him but I didn't want his blood on my hands. So, I told them to let him go. If he survived in the forest it would be his own good luck, and if a tiger ate him...well, that was his fate. So, we left the door of the bamboo hut open and by the next morning, he was gone, escaping into the jungle on his own....

The dacoit cocked his head and shrugged, the perspiration running down his face. 'Who knows, Mughlai bhai, maybe that boy was you?'

Yusuf stopped again and this time I could hear a sound too, the rumble of a jeep's engine somewhere outside. He held up one hand, warning me to keep still. We heard a door slam shut and then another vehicle approaching. I could see from the expression on his face that Yusuf knew the police had arrived, though all he said to me was, 'Go bring me the Miss Sahib's guns.'

Thinking back on that day, so many years later, I often wonder how much of what I did was instinctual and whether I was even aware of the consequences of my actions. Or was it simply something that happened outside myself, as if I were watching a film?

My memories are more like photographs in a book than a movie unspooling on a screen.

> As I stand up from the charpoy, Yusuf reaches for his rifle and I see him cradling it across his lap. Stepping through the door into the Miss Sahib's bedroom, I hear voices outside, as if someone is arguing. Running into the living room, I catch sight of the tiger skin on the wall with bands of light falling across its tawny coat. Turning towards the dufter door, I can see one corner of the steel cupboard where the rifle and shotgun are kept. It is locked but I know that the key is in the top drawer of the Miss Sahib's desk. Glancing to my left, I realize that the front door is unlatched. Through the rusty screens I can see two police jeeps outside and men with guns.
>
> 'Daniel!' Miss Cranston screams. I see her racing out of the shade of a neem tree and across the bright pool of sunlight that fills the dusty yard. Though she is coming to get me the Miss Sahib doesn't seem

to be moving, like a running figure in a photograph. I turn towards her and push my way out between the screen doors, hearing them clap behind me like a trap. The glare of sunlight beyond the edge of the verandah is blinding after being indoors. Policemen aim their rifles at us. Somebody shouts a warning but I can't make out the words. Then I run into the light and the Miss Sahib picks me up in her arms. A couple of policemen grab us roughly and drag us behind a jeep. After that, pressing myself against Miss Cranston, I close my eyes and there is nothing but sounds. Running feet. A voice calls out, as if through a loudspeaker. The first gunshot. A long silence. Then a volley of bullets. I hear Miss Cranston sigh, a soft sound from deep inside that makes me hold onto her more tightly than before. After that, there are more gunshots...more than I can count, like a string of firecrackers going off.

When I finally opened my eyes, I saw a policeman being supported by two others, with blood streaming down one arm. He was walking but had to be helped into a jeep, which drove away quickly, taking him to a hospital. Moments later, Miss Cranston stood up and I slipped from her arms. Shanti Ayah and Amos came over and helped me get to my feet as a police officer carrying a revolver stepped out of the bungalow, followed by three other men with rifles. One of them was smiling, as if nothing had happened, as if it were all just a game.

The senior police officer came across to Miss Cranston and spoke to her in a coarse, angry voice, asking if she knew the man inside. She nodded, her face as pale as I had ever seen it.

'What was his name?' the officer demanded.

'Joseph,' she said.

'Did you know he was a criminal?'

'Yes,' she said. 'He used to live here in the children's home when he was a boy. This was where he grew up.'

'Is that why you protected him?' The policeman was shouting at her.

'He came to me for help,' she said. 'He was injured.'

The police officer pointed his pistol at her as he spoke.

'He killed three of my men and murdered another three innocent victims day before yesterday. He has twenty-seven murders against his name and for fifteen years, he's been running away from us. Now he's dead and no one can protect him, not even you!'

The police officer turned and spat on the ground beside him, then gestured for his men to arrest the Miss Sahib. She didn't resist as they took her by both arms and walked her across to their jeep, making her sit in the back. As Shanti Ayah held me I wanted to call out but no sound came from my mouth, as if my tongue had been cut. When they drove away, the tyres kicking up plumes of dust, the only thought in my head was that Miss Cranston would be hanged.

III
SOMEPLACE LIKE HOME

ONE

Before sunrise, I slip out of my room and climb the brick staircase at the back of the bungalow, onto the broad, flat roof overlooking the compound. By the time I got here last evening, it was already dusk and there were so many people, questions, laughter, tears of reunion, I didn't get a chance to take in the place itself. Now I can see some of the changes, a new row of small homes built along the back wall, each with its own square patch of yard in front, punctuated by a papaya tree, or a thorn hedge. The other buildings look much the same except for the dish antennae that sprout like mushrooms from every roof. The two tall brick chimneys of the old sugar mill are still standing, though the top of one has broken off. I cannot see the cemetery from here but it seems as if the jungle of lantana still separates the graves from the ruins.

A faint, unpleasant odour taints the air—like a hint of decomposing flesh mixed with a sickly bouquet of fermentation—carried on the breeze from one of the sugar refineries to the north of the compound. The distant stench, which I remember from my childhood, mingles with other familiar morning smells, the subtle perfume of a trumpet-flower vine clambering up a trellis, covering one corner of the bungalow's front verandah, as well as the dry, sweet scent of dust and the oniony fragrance of neem trees with their clusters of tiny green fruit. One of the branches reaches the edge of the roof and I break off a twig. Chewing the end and spitting out bits of bark, I gnaw at the neem twig, remembering how we used to brush our teeth with these sticks. Its bitter taste assails my tongue as saliva fills my mouth.

Last night, we stayed up late, eating dinner around ten o'clock, when Pradeep could see that I was fading. He and his wife live in one half of the main bungalow, along with their two sons, one of whom is married and has a daughter of his own. They insisted on vacating my old room, so that I could sleep in there, while the family crowded into the master bedroom and the hall behind it. Their part of the house includes what used to be the living room, which has been partitioned to make a separate kitchen, though I am still disoriented by the layout, trying to get my bearings.

Stepping out of the taxi yesterday, I recognized Pradeep immediately, even before he stood up, supporting himself with an aluminium crutch because of his withered leg. He has put on weight, but so have I, though the mischievous expression on his face hasn't changed. We embraced and he leaned against me, almost knocking me over. His wife grew up here too, though I can't place her. She was one of the younger orphans and says she remembers me. Her name is Bimla.

'You're the one we used to call "Jungli",' she said, laughing, as Pradeep tried to hush her with a wave of his hand.

The granddaughter, four years old, watched me with suspicious curiosity, as her mother, the daughter-in-law, brought me a glass of water from the fridge.

'How is the electricity supply these days?' I asked, noticing a TV in one corner of the room. It was a meaningless question, an excuse for me to keep talking.

'Better than it used to be,' said Pradeep, 'but in summer there is load shedding and we have an inverter to keep the fans going.'

We spoke English mostly and when I switched to Hindi, Pradeep smirked.

'You talk like an Angrez!' He teased me.

'That's what I've become...an Am'rikan.'

We laughed, as if it were an old joke that we'd forgotten.

Pradeep explained that the compound is now a Christian colony. Almost a hundred people live here, many of them descendants of the staff who worked at CMCH and some of the orphans like him and Bimla.

'Once the Miss Sahib left, the money from the mission stopped coming in. We had no idea what would happen next. People picked up whatever work they could. The Children's Home closed but Master Ezekiel Masih opened a school and villagers nearby began to send their children. Others started raising chickens or pigs. Some drove trucks and jeeps. What could we do? People have to eat.'

'How about you?' I asked.

Pradeep shrugged and smiled. 'In the beginning there was nothing for me to do. With this leg of mine, nobody expected me to go very far. But Masterji encouraged me to study and sent me to college in Lucknow. I came back as a teacher in his school. When he died, poor man, I became the principal.'

'How many students are in the school?' I asked.

'Two hundred and sixty-four,' he replied, with a grin. 'This year twenty-seven out of thirty students in Class Ten passed the Board Exams and seven of them got a first division.'

'That's wonderful. Congratulations!' I said.

He clasped my hand affectionately.

Pradeep's younger son, Michael, is studying chemical engineering in Delhi though he is home for the holidays.

'Uncle,' he asked me, 'Are you a professor at MIT?'

I shook my head and smiled.

'No. I look after one of the laboratories,' I said. 'I'm a facility supervisor.'

'What kind of lab is it?' Pradeep asked.

'It's called the J. D. Wallace Environmental Engineering Center, where scientists research the effects of climate change and other related problems.'

It was strange for me to be surrounded by an extended family, three generations, all in the same room. Living in Cambridge, I seldom meet anyone other than my colleagues and a few friends, usually one or two at a time. My partner, Nadia and I share an apartment but each of us has our own room and routines, guarding our privacy even though we live together. But with Pradeep's family it seems as if everyone occupies the same space without any boundaries between them. The portion of the living room where we gathered is filled with furniture, including a divan that is used as a bed. A low dining table stands in one corner, on which our dinner was served. Pradeep and I ate first. There was no cutlery and Bimla noticed me hesitate after she put a plate in front of me.

'Shall I bring you a spoon?' she asked.

Shaking my head, I replied, 'No, I'll eat with my fingers, though it's been a while and I might make a mess.'

The others waited until we had finished before helping themselves, though Bimla got a plate for her granddaughter and fed her, forming each mouthful with her fingers and urging the girl to eat. Seated in their midst, I felt self-conscious at first but also completely at home.

The hunting trophies have all been taken down, except for a single set of blackbuck horns, high up on the wall. The roshandan is still there, just below the ceiling but other than that the room has been rearranged completely. There are a few family photographs on a side table and a framed picture of Jesus with a gilded halo around his head. A plaque on the wall, decorated with an image of pink roses, bears a Bible verse:

> Love is patient, love is kind. It does not envy, it does not boast, it is not proud. It does not dishonour others, it is not self-seeking, it is not easily angered, it keeps no record of wrongs. (Corinthians 13: 4-5).

Everything seems a little smaller than I recall, more crowded and more cluttered. My old room has changed as well and there are two other beds pushed up against the walls and a couple of steel cupboards. Again, it seems as if the family has filled every space with hardly any room left for my suitcase. Lying in the dark last night, I could hear whispers from next door, a child's laughter and Pradeep grumbling about something. Unlike the gloomy silences that I recall from my childhood, the entire building seemed alive as I drifted off into a dreamless sleep.

Now, this morning, as I stand on the roof of the bungalow and watch the pariah kites gliding past on outstretched wings and hear a rooster cry, I am happy to be alone for a while, to absorb the sounds and smells that I remember from when I was a boy. Somewhere a diesel pump starts up and then dies with a consumptive cough. A truck horn hoots in the distance, like an alarm call. A chorus of birdsong surrounds me, though I have forgotten most of the names Miss Cranston taught us, except for the coppersmith barbet, with its tapping, metallic cry.

I wonder, if we had stayed here, would I still be living in this house? Maybe I would have married one of the girls from the Children's Home and filled these rooms with sons and daughters. The Miss Sahib might have become a grandmother and things would have gone on, just as they had before. Who knows? Perhaps, I would have run away instead, escaping to some other town or city, or maybe back into the forest out of which I came.

From below, I hear Pradeep calling my name. The rising sun is blazing through the branches of the neem tree and someone is ringing a cycle bell at the gate. As I descend the staircase, Pradeep is waiting on the verandah.

'What were you doing up there?' he asks. 'Let's have some tea.'

Soon Bimla appears and brings us each a steaming glass of chai. It is too hot for me to hold and I set it down, balanced on the arm of my chair. Pradeep watches me with a look that I remember well, his eyes guarded but amused, as if he is about to play a practical joke on me.

'You slept well?' he asks.

'I did, but because of my jet lag, I woke up early.'

'Yes, of course. It must be night-time in America,' he says. 'I was trying to explain it to Sarita, my granddaughter. She couldn't understand. "Why does the sun go to the other side of the world?"'

'You are lucky to have such a wonderful family,' I tell him.

He nods, serious for a moment.

'Of course, I am,' he replies. 'You never wanted a family of your own?'

'Not really,' I say. 'I live with someone...though she and I aren't married.'

Pradeep sips his tea with a soft slurping sound.

'What's her name?' he asks.

'Nadia,' I say, meeting his gaze. 'She's originally from Egypt.'

'Is she Muslim or Christian?' he asks.

'Neither,' I say. 'She's an atheist like me.'

Pradeep looks away for a moment, absorbing what I've said.

'I'm glad you have someone,' he says, then hesitates. 'But we won't tell the others. They wouldn't understand—not believing in God and living with someone who isn't your wife is like the sun going around to the other side of the earth....'

'Okay,' I agree and shrug.

After I take a sip of the thick, sweet tea, blowing on it first to cool it down, I let the silence between us extend for another few breaths.

'It's good to be back,' I say.

'Why didn't you come earlier?' A mild note of accusation enters his voice. 'Fifty years is much too long.'

'I didn't think anyone would remember me.'

He exhales impatiently. 'You forgot us. We didn't forget you.'

'No,' I say. 'It wasn't like that at all. I didn't forget but there was no chance of coming back. I had to move on...'

'The Miss Sahib wrote, but you never did.' His voice isn't angry or resentful though there is a hint of sadness and gentle recrimination.

'I should have written but what would I have said?'

Pradeep reaches over and brushes his hand over my arm.

'Forget it,' he says. 'The important thing is that you are here.'

'Eight years ago, I promised Miss Cranston that I would come back and bring her ashes to be buried in Shakkarganj,' I explain. 'She was already losing her memory by then. Within a year, she didn't know who I was, though she still remembered this place. At the end of her life, the only language she spoke was Hindustani. She would say random things like: "Mujhe bewakoof mat samjho! Dood mein paani zaroor milaya hai!" Don't treat me like a fool. I know you've added water to the milk!'

Pradeep laughs. 'Yes, I remember. She always accused the dairywallah of mixing water with the milk he delivered!'

Then he looks at his hands. 'It must have been difficult for you, losing her like that, slowly, one memory after another.'

'I wasn't with her most of the time. We'd had our disagreements and I moved away when I was nineteen,' I tell him. 'For more than twenty years we didn't speak until I finally thought I should go and see her. She welcomed me back without resentment but it could never be the same. Now that she's gone I feel the loss much more, as if I should have been a better son to her.'

'At least you had a mother to mourn,' Pradeep replies. Again, there is no bitterness, though the abruptness of his words takes me by surprise. 'Why did you stop speaking to her?' he asks.

'A lot of reasons,' I reply. 'I had a tough time moving to America, trying to fit in, and I resented the choices she made for me when I was younger, which had consequences later on that I thought were unfair. She couldn't understand why I was so rebellious....'

I pause for a minute, to let my mind catch up with my words but Pradeep remains silent, which is his way of urging me to keep talking.

'There was other stuff too. I didn't want anything to do with her church and I told her I didn't believe in God. But more than that, I don't think I ever accepted the Miss Sahib as my mother. It's a strange thing to say, but I wasn't grateful to her for adopting me, though most people probably think I should have been. Of course, she was always generous, even when we didn't have much money, but there was a quiet condescension in her manner...all gentle and sweet but laced with underlying expectations that I would do as I was told.'

'Did you fight with her?' Pradeep asks.

'Not really. No,' I say. 'I mean, we argued sometimes and I would get so angry I'd stay in my room for a couple of days, refusing to come out. But she never really fought back, at least not directly. Either she would pray about it or ask me to forgive her, though what she actually meant was that she was forgiving me...'

'But you left home?'

'I went away to college and never came back. That was sort of how it happened. You see, she was teaching at a Christian boarding school, North Shore Bible Academy, where she had an apartment on campus. I attended the public high school before going to college. After I left home, I just didn't want to deal with her any more.'

'She must have been heartbroken,' Pradeep says.

'I imagine she was,' I agree. 'During my first year of college, she used to write me letters, which I never read or answered, though I cashed the checks she always enclosed. Once she drove across to see me in Amherst but I asked my roommates to tell her I wasn't there. I know, I was being cruel, but I was going through a lot myself and I just wanted a clean break from my past.'

Beyond the low hedge that separates the bungalow from the driveway, I can see a man sweeping leaves, his arm moving rhythmically, as he squats on his haunches, wielding the broom like a bristling sword.

'How long have you lived in this house?' I ask Pradeep.

He thinks for a moment. 'Thirty years, almost,' he says. 'Since Bimla and I were married. For a long time, the bungalow lay empty because we expected the Miss Sahib to return but then she wrote and said that there was no chance that she would come back and we should do whatever we wanted with the property. Eventually, after negotiating with the mission lawyers, Ezekiel Masih and some of the elders marked out plots for each of the families. There was some disagreement but generally it was done fairly and peacefully. Masterji and his wife moved into one half of the bungalow—the other side—and this part was kept as staff quarters for the school. When we got married, soon after I began teaching, this was the accommodation we were given.'

'What happened to all the hunting trophies?' I ask.

'Bimla didn't like them being here, so we took them down. For a while they were kept in the science room at the school but eventually they fell apart and were thrown away. Most of the furniture remained but over the years it has broken and things have been replaced.'

'What about the Miss Sahib's guns?'

'I heard that the police took those after they killed Yusuf Daku,' he says. 'Nobody ever saw them again. What use would they have been to us?'

Moments later, his daughter-in-law comes out and picks up the empty glasses from beside our chairs. For the first time, I notice a mongrel lying in the yard, its fur the same colour as the dust. I catch sight of the dog when it lifts a hind paw to scratch its ear.

'The water should be hot for your bath. We turned the geyser on an hour ago,' says Pradeep, hoisting himself awkwardly out of his chair and reaching for his crutch. He smiles at me. 'Daniel, if there's anything you need....'

'Thank you,' I reply.

'We'll have breakfast and then we'll go to church at ten.'

'Is it Sunday?' I say, surprised. 'Yes, of course, it is.'

Two hours later, I am sitting on one of the hard, wooden pews in the chapel, just as I did every Sunday as a child, listening to the wheezing, reedy notes of an old pump organ as the congregation rises to sing a hymn. I haven't been to church for more than forty years, other than attending a couple of weddings and the christening of a colleague's child. As Pradeep and I walked across from the bungalow to the chapel, accompanied by his family, I was greeted by more than a dozen people, each of whom said they had known me when I was a boy. Most of them, I didn't recognize but they had obviously heard that I was coming and offered condolences. Their voices were full of emotion and I could tell that the Miss Sahib was still remembered with fondness, half a century after her departure.

The chapel is no different from what I recall, bare whitewashed walls and fluorescent tube lights. Long-stemmed ceiling fans hang over the pews and there is a hymn board on one wall, displaying the numbers of hymns to be sung. A large wooden cross is positioned over the altar, which is covered with a lace cloth. The men are seated on one side and women on the other. Before the service,

Pradeep introduced me to the pastor, Reverend Raju Nazareth, a squat, energetic man, who told me that he was related to Amos, the senior aide at CMCH when I was a boy. There are at least a hundred people in the congregation, the entire Christian community of Shakkarganj, and I am aware that they are watching me with curiosity and anticipation.

Before preaching his sermon, Reverend Nazareth welcomes me as 'our brother, Daniel, who has returned from America'. Most of the service is conducted in Hindi but for my benefit he speaks this part in English and there are murmurs of greeting all around me. My first impression is that the pastor is self-righteous and insincere, though I try to restrain my prejudices. During the final prayer, he thanks God for bringing me home and asks that Jesus 'shower his blessings upon me.'

Following the service, tea and biscuits are served under the eucalyptus trees next to the front steps. One by one, the congregants approach and shake my hand, introducing themselves. A few of the names come back to me and a couple of faces but mostly it is their gestures and words that are familiar, not the people themselves.

'Can you still speak Hindi?' asks an elderly man, the son of Shambu Bearer.

'A little,' I say, self-consciously. 'But I haven't spoken Hindi for a long time.'

He tilts his head to one side, then asks if I have children.

'I'm afraid not,' I reply, shaking my head.

'I have twelve,' he tells me proudly, then leans closer. 'My first wife gave me seven. After she died, I married again. With the second, I have five.'

'Congratulations,' I say, as he totters off.

A woman in a bright green sari with gilt embroidery asks me where I live in America. When I say Boston, she tells me that her son is in Fort Worth, Texas. Promising to give me his address, she explains that he is a software engineer.

Others ask about the Miss Sahib and why she never came back.

'She would have certainly come back, if she'd had a choice, but the Indian Consulate wouldn't give her a visa. She applied at least three times,' I say.

'How long are you staying?' another woman asks.

'Just a week.'

'Only?'

I've never spoken to so many people in a single morning and by the end of it, I am exhausted. Half of them have invited me to their homes for a meal or tea and I keep saying, 'You're very kind but I'm only here for a short time.' Finally, Pradeep rescues me, as the congregation begins to drift away.

'We should go and see the cemetery,' he suggests. 'That way, you can decide where the Miss Sahib's grave should be dug.'

Reverend Nazareth joins us, still wearing his cassock, as we make our way behind the chapel and across the old canal that used to irrigate the gardens, though the narrow channel of crumbling concrete is dry and full of leaves.

'We now have water piped in,' Pradeep tells me, negotiating the obstacle with difficulty. Beyond the canal is the jungle of lantana, with orange and yellow flowers. Its pungent fragrance comes from the leaves as much as the blossoms.

Miss Cranston once told me how her father had acquired this property. The old sugar mill was one of the first of its kind, built back in the 1830s by Eamon Lynch, an Irishman who persuaded the farmers in this region to start growing sugar cane. He produced gur and shakkar, which is how the village of Shakkarganj got its name but he also opened a distillery and made rum that was sold to the East India Company army. It was a profitable business for a while and the Irishman bought up a lot of land in the area and became a prominent zamindar. He also married two village women, which scandalized the British, though both of them converted and became Roman Catholics. Before Lynch died of typhoid at the age of forty-eight, he had two sons, one by each of his wives.

After his death the two women quarrelled and there was a legal battle over his property that was fought all the way to the High Court in Allahabad. The dispute outlasted Lynch's wives and his sons carried on with the court cases for more than fifty years until they both went bankrupt. Of course, the sugar mill and distillery had gone out of business by then because it couldn't compete with more modern factories. By the time Reverend and Mrs Cranston came to India in 1923, the two brothers were also dead and the only surviving member of the family was an illegitimate daughter that one of Eamon Lynch's wives gave birth to after his death. She was living by herself in the bungalow, which was in a terrible state of disrepair. In the end, the Miss Sahib's father bought the whole place for ten thousand rupees, which was donated by a couple of churches back in America.

Cutting through the underbrush, a dirt path leads to a wrought iron gate and a wire mesh fence that encloses the cemetery. There are many more graves than I remember and Pradeep points out Shanti Ayah's headstone.

'She was like a mother to me,' he says, softly.

At the far corner of the cemetery, three marble slabs lie side by side, marking Reverend and Mrs Cranston's graves, with their son Ricky between them. The inscriptions have eroded though I can just make out the names.

'Where would you like her to be?' Reverend Nazareth asks, then adds in a disapproving tone, 'Usually, we don't permit the burial of ashes. Cremation is a Hindu custom, not ours. But in your mother's case, I can't refuse.'

I look at him then look away.

'It doesn't really matter, which side she's on,' I say, 'does it?'

'Here would be best,' Pradeep suggests, pointing with his crutch to the left, on the far side of Reverend Cranston's headstone.

'That's fine.' I nod. 'I don't think she would have had a preference. All I know is that she wanted to be buried here.'

The reverend places a solicitous hand on my shoulder.

'Don't worry, Brother Daniel, she will rest in peace,' he says in a pious, sanctimonious voice.

TWO

Three weeks after the police raided CMCH and killed Yusuf Daku, one of the missionary doctors from the hospital in Amrudpur came across to fetch me and we drove away together in the Miss Sahib's jeep. He explained that I would be going with him to Delhi and that the US Embassy had arranged for me to meet my mother and fly out with her to America. The day before I left, Shanti Ayah helped me pack a suitcase, which contained a few of my clothes, while the rest was filled with some of Miss Cranston's dresses, shoes, and other belongings. Following her arrest, I had moved back into the boys' dormitory and didn't return to the bungalow until the day before I left Shakkarganj. My bedroom had been cleaned up and there was no sign of blood, though there were bullet holes in the walls, as if someone had chipped the plaster away with a chisel. Though Shanti Ayah was with me, I still felt uneasy stepping through the front door into the shadowy rooms, almost expecting to hear Yusuf's voice calling out to me again.

In Delhi, I was taken to the airport in the middle of the night and one of the officials from the embassy escorted me through immigration, where several policemen studied my passport and asked me questions. Through an inner window, I could see other passengers waiting in a large room with rows of chairs. Miss Cranston was among them, sitting alone with a worried look on her face. Eventually, the policemen and immigration officers opened a door and let me through. For a moment I held back, wondering what would happen next but then the Miss Sahib saw me and got up from her chair and ran across to hug me. I was shaking, as if I had a fever but she held me close and stroked my hair. All the other passengers in the departure lounge were watching us but I didn't care.

After that, I remember hearing an announcement over the loudspeaker and we walked out onto the tarmac. Climbing a staircase, I heard the roar of another jet taking off before we boarded our plane. The man from the embassy came with us all the way to the door of the aircraft where he shook my hand encouragingly. When we took off, I was terrified but Miss Cranston kept her arm around me. Over the next two days and nights, we had a long sequence of flights from Delhi, via Tehran, Istanbul, Geneva, and London to New York.

Once I was sure that we were safe and I got used to the humming drone of the airplanes, I asked the Miss Sahib where the police had taken her. She said they had put her in the district jail in Bareilly to begin with, in a special section for female prisoners, but after the US Embassy got involved, she was moved to a detention centre in Delhi, which was a little more comfortable. The police kept her locked up for two-and-a-half weeks, until the mission lawyers and consular officials were able to negotiate her deportation. All of this, she explained to me in a quiet, matter-of-fact manner, simplifying the details and leaving out things I wouldn't understand or that might upset me. Though she made it sound as if it wasn't an unpleasant experience, I could tell that it must have been frightening and traumatic. Many years later, I was able to piece together more of the story from files and other documents she'd kept. Several times, during our journey, I saw tears forming in the corners of her eyes as she held me against her with trembling hands.

After we reached America, we took a train from New York to Boston. One of the churches in Peabody, Massachusetts, which supported CMCH, came to our rescue and gave us shelter. All we had with us was the contents of our suitcase. Two women from the church had stocked the kitchen with groceries and took us shopping at JCPenney's, where I got a pair of jeans and a couple of spare shirts. There wasn't a single book in the apartment and very little furniture, just beds and a table with two chairs in the kitchen, as well as an old desk that leaned to one side. I remember Miss Cranston propped it up with a can of tuna fish wedged underneath one leg. She always had a solution for problems like that.

At this point, she was still convinced that we would be able to go back to India and all her energies were focused on our return. She asked the people at the church for a typewriter, so that she could write letters to the authorities in India, as well as the US Embassy, the mission headquarters and other supporting churches. Unlike the old Remington in her dufter back home, this typewriter was a portable Underwood, a compact machine in a sleek case that snapped shut so you could carry it around. Those first few weeks we hardly went out of the apartment, except to attend church and to the post office to mail letters. It was summer and the air in Massachusetts was almost as humid as it had been in Shakkarganj. I knew that the ocean was close by but we only went to see it six or seven months later, after the Miss Sahib got a car, a rusty Ford Fairlane that someone in the church gave her. Before that, another member of the congregation had given us a black and white TV. I began to watch cartoons and other shows obsessively, blocking out all the uncertainty and upheaval in our lives.

My only happy memory of that summer of 1967 was when Walt Disney's *The Jungle Book* opened. The Miss Sahib and I walked down to the Strand Theatre on Main Street in Peabody and stood in line for almost an hour to get tickets for the matinee. It was a hot summer day and I was restless but once we entered the theatre and settled into our seats, it was as if I'd been hypnotized. That was the first movie I ever saw for there was no cinema in Shakkarganj. As soon as Mowgli made his appearance, rescued by Bagheera, I glanced up at Miss Cranston with a puzzled expression. A few minutes later, when he imitated the howling of the wolf cubs, I could see a smile on her face. Soon enough, we were both laughing at their playful antics and the comical scenes with Baloo the bear.

After we watched the movie the first time, I kept pestering the Miss Sahib to take me back to see it again and again. She had to make up excuses because we didn't have much money. Tickets only cost a dollar back then but that was more than she could afford.

Altogether, we probably watched *The Jungle Book* five or six times and I learned all the songs by heart. Of course, the setting wasn't anything like the India we'd known but there was something familiar in the caricatures of the animals and scenes in the forest that made us forget where we were, at least for an hour or so.

From morning until evening, Miss Cranston would sit at her desk, fingers flying over the typewriter keys, as letters emerged one after the other. At some point she got a telephone installed and once or twice she tried to call India, raising her voice as if the distance itself made her words inaudible. She spoke to operators in Hindustani, trying to get through to Shakkarganj. There was a phone in her dufter but it seemed to have been disconnected. Eventually, she got through to someone in Amrudpur but the person on the other end of the line didn't have any information. Gradually, a few letters began to arrive at the apartment, aerogrammes from India addressed in blue ink. She told me very little of what was going on, maybe because she didn't want me to worry after all we'd been through. For me, the television took the place of the stories she used to read to me. In the evenings I would curl up beside her on the sofa and we would watch whatever came on, reruns of westerns and game shows where they gave away cars and refrigerators as prizes. Because it was summer, I didn't have to attend school and Miss Cranston kept insisting that we would be on our way back to India by the end of August, though somehow I knew that wasn't going to happen.

Later on, after I enrolled in middle school and went off every morning by bus, struggling to make it through each day in a new world of strange voices, loud buzzers signalling the end of class, cafeteria trays and teachers who couldn't understand me when I spoke, I began to hope that we might return to India despite my fears and violent memories of the police encounter.

At the same time, I knew that the Miss Sahib was losing hope and I could see a disheartened look in her eyes when I came home from school, as her letters remained unanswered or she got discouraging news. Through all of this, the typewriter remained her refuge and as long as she was tapping on the keys it seemed as if there might be some chance we'd return.

Eventually, after we'd been in Peabody for six months, I came home one day to see her sitting at the desk, its leg still propped up with the tuna fish can. She was typing furiously and when I came in, she called out, 'Mowgli, there's a snack on the kitchen counter!'

I helped myself to the peanut butter sandwich she'd made for me and walked over to the desk. She had a stack of papers on one side and was rolling another two sheets into the typewriter with a piece of carbon paper between them.

'What's that?' I asked. 'More letters?'

'No,' she replied with a shy sort of smile. 'I'm writing a story for you. It's a new Jungle Book.'

When I looked at her with a confused expression, she laughed.

'Is it my story?' I asked.

'No, of course not,' she said, 'though it's set in Hathi Talao Wildlife Sanctuary, where you were found. I've tried to imagine what it might have been like for a boy to be raised in the wild. But it's all made up.'

'How will it end?' I asked.

She shrugged.

'I don't know,' she said. 'Maybe I'll never finish the story, because I don't want it to end.'

'Does he leave the forest, like in the movie?' I asked.

'What do you think should happen?' she said, putting her hand on my shoulder.

'It doesn't matter,' I answered, 'if it's just a story.'

❧

A year later, when it became obvious that we wouldn't be going back to Shakkarganj, Miss Cranston got a job at North Shore Bible Academy. We moved into a new apartment at the school, away from town. Though I could have joined the academy, I chose to stay in the public school and rode the bus each day. Soon after we moved, the Miss Sahib wrote to Master Ezekiel Masih and asked him to collect the files from her cabinets and other documents from the desk drawers. Many of these were family letters going back to her childhood, correspondence with the Mission Board and Foreigners Registration Office, as well as my files and adoption papers. One of the missionaries from the hospital in Amrudpur helped sort and pack things up, then had it shipped by sea freight in an old steamer trunk, which the Miss Sahib's parents had used when they first sailed to India.

The trunk arrived six months later, delivered by two men in a van who struggled up the stairs and set it down in the middle of our living room. When Miss Cranston opened it, I had no interest to see what it contained. By then I was already a belligerent teenager trying to come to terms with America. The last thing I wanted was a reminder of home. The Miss Sahib opened the trunk and took out the contents slowly, methodically, with a sad look in her eyes, reading some of the papers and flipping through the files and photograph albums. After she emptied the trunk, Miss Cranston put everything back in again and closed the lid, locking it up. She then dragged the heavy chest into a cupboard in her bedroom, where it remained out of sight.

For many years, I completely forgot about the steamer trunk. After I went away to college, I gradually began to shut the Miss Sahib out of my life. She tried to keep in touch with me but there had always been an undercurrent in our relationship that made me angry, her unspoken demands and pious Christianity, which I rejected. Mostly, though, I resented having been taken away from a place and people I knew, where I had struggled to be accepted and finally felt at home. Now I had to start all over again. Miss Cranston did whatever she could to try and help me but I was at an age when everything seemed hopeless and unfair. Her gestures of love and affection only made my hostility worse and the few times I came back to the apartment, during college, I would get depressed and miserable.

After graduating from UMass, I finally cut myself off from the Miss Sahib completely and moved into a rented house in New

Hampshire with a couple of college friends. We worked together at a factory in Manchester, where we assembled baby carriages for two dollars and ten cents an hour. It was a miserable job but I finally felt independent and free of my past. The uncertainty and hand-to-mouth existence didn't bother me at all for I had broken loose from the Miss Sahib's protective, maternal embrace. Though there were times when I missed the sound of her voice, our separation gave me the confidence that I could survive on my own.

When I think back on that period of my life, I'm ashamed by some of the things I did but I also feel it was necessary for me to break away from Miss Cranston and start a new life, no matter how irresponsible and unsettled it was. Sometimes I felt lost and abandoned but at the same time there was a strange sort of freedom in having no past, no family, no point of origin. In college, I remember telling a girlfriend once that I was an orphan and she looked at me with a weird expression, as if she didn't understand.

'Do you think you'll ever find your real parents?' she asked.

I shook my head. 'It's not going to happen.'

'But wouldn't you want to know?' she insisted.

'Maybe. Maybe not,' I replied.

'I hate my parents,' she said. 'But at least I know who they are.'

We split up soon after that and I decided it was simpler to invent a story for myself and for others, explaining how I'd come to America with my parents who emigrated here from India. During my freshman year, I took an Introduction to Psychology course and we were asked to write a paper on the subject, 'Who Am I?' The professor was obsessed with 'nature vs. nurture' and I knew that if I told the truth he would surely call on me in class and make a point of excavating my psyche, so I wrote what ended up being the first draft of the story I've embellished ever since. My parents were immigrants from India, and our home was in Delhi. They had been hired by a pharmaceutical company in Burlington and we came to America when I was twelve. Soon after our arrival, my father died of a stroke and my mother raised me on her own until I was nineteen, when she was killed in an air crash, while flying to a conference in Minnesota. The professor gave me an 'A' on the paper and wrote a long comment, saying how he was impressed that I could 'recount the trauma and loss of my parents with such maturity and insight'.

After that I made up different versions of the story, explaining to anyone who asked that my parents were scientists who'd been recruited to work at Boston University but a couple of years after we arrived in the US, both of them died in a car crash on Route 95...or my mother got brain cancer and my father was so upset he had a heart attack. Depending on who was listening, I made up new elements of the story and it didn't really matter if I contradicted myself. In America, people will believe almost anything, though they want a complete story, with a beginning, middle, and end. Americans like to be assured that everything adds up. As I quickly discovered, it was easier to lie about my origins than to try and explain the things I didn't know about myself. Even when I got my first full-time job, working as a salesman for a heating oil company, I made up most of the details on the job application and I remember telling the woman in human resources how my parents were chemical engineers, which is how I got interested in the petroleum industry.

Often, I made a joke of it but other times there was a real need to construct a personal narrative that made it seem as if I actually belonged here, justifying my presence in America. For some reason, in most of these personal fictions that I concocted, my parents always died sudden and often violent deaths. Obviously, Miss Cranston played no role in my imaginary biographies.

By the time I landed my current job at MIT, where I've worked for the past twenty-three years, there wasn't much need for me to make up things on my résumé because most employers had stopped asking personal questions. If I met someone for the first time, in a bar or at a friend's wedding, I dodged the subject of family as best I could but if they really pressed me, I could easily retrieve one or another of the many lies I'd used before.

The only person I've told the truth to is Nadia. But even with her, I began by hiding the facts. She works at the Boston Public

Library in the rare books section. We met through a mutual friend, who introduced us and I asked her to have a drink with me at a place on Newbury Street called The Governor's Table, which isn't there any more. After that we started dating and when things began to get serious, I eventually confessed and told her the real story, or as much of it as I know, about being a foundling rescued from the jungle. She listened quietly, as she always does, without interrupting or asking questions. It was a strange feeling, having hidden the truth for so many years, to finally open up about the unknown aspects of my life as well as the story of my adoption.

Ultimately, Nadia was the one who persuaded me to get back in touch with Miss Cranston, after a gap of twenty years. She even came with me to see her the first time I went back to her apartment. I was surprised how well they got along, though the two of them are quite different in many ways. The Miss Sahib was still the strong-willed, independent person that I remembered, though she looked older and her shoulders were starting to stoop. Nadia is strong in a different sort of way, quieter and gentler, with a more reserved manner. She doesn't express her opinions directly, though she has firm beliefs as well as doubts. If it wasn't for her, I would have just carried on avoiding my past instead of being reconciled to the truth.

My relationship with Miss Cranston could never be the same, though I think she still thought of me as her son. The distance I'd put between us remained. Nadia reassured me that it was okay to maintain a level of separation even after we were reunited. She herself had gone through a lot of issues with her family, who weren't particularly conservative but didn't like the idea that she was 'happily apostate', as she liked to say. By this time, I was older and less rebellious and resentful. Though Miss Cranston would never be a mother to me, there remained a bond between us and I made a point of visiting her at least three or four times a year. She came to our apartment too, on several occasions and seemed pleased to see how civilized and domesticated I'd become.

One year, Nadia and I had her over for Thanksgiving and it seemed almost as if we were a family. Though she lived alone, the

Miss Sahib had plenty of friends from church as well as the school where she taught.

'I don't come into Cambridge often,' she said, looking out the window at the Charles River and the Boston skyline, which we can see from our living room. 'It feels like another country to me.'

'Do you ever cook Indian food?' I asked her.

She shook her head. 'No. But there's a Nepali restaurant in Peabody that delivers and some of it's okay.'

'Daniel cooks a great dal and chicken curry,' Nadia said.

'Really?' Miss Cranston looked surprised. 'How did you learn to do that?'

'I got a cookbook and followed the instructions,' I said.

She raised her eyebrows as if she didn't quite believe me, then changed the subject.

'Why don't the two of you get married?' she asked, with her usual forthright abruptness.

I was concerned that Nadia might take offence but she just laughed.

'Neither of us believes in marriage,' she said, taking the turkey out of the oven. 'It's not our thing.'

Miss Cranston didn't react for a minute. She was drinking cranberry juice, while we had opened a bottle of Malbec.

'Still,' she said, after a long pause. 'It would be nice.'

'But you never married,' Nadia replied. 'Did you, Elizabeth?'

It was something I could never have said but Nadia has none of my hang-ups. She'd started using the Miss Sahib's first name, right from the start.

'I was engaged once,' Miss Cranston replied. 'Though I've never told anyone before.'

She smiled when I looked at her in surprise.

'When was this?' Nadia asked.

'Right after I finished college. His name was Bruce Ransome. He'd been in the army and came back from the war, studying at Boston University. We met during my senior year and he proposed to me just before graduation.'

'What happened?' I asked. 'Why didn't you get married?'

'A month after we got engaged, a telegram arrived from my father, saying that my mother had died of a stroke,' Miss Cranston explained. 'I decided to go back to India and be with him for a couple of months. But once I returned to Shakkarganj, it was obvious that my father wouldn't be able to run the Children's Home on his own. That's when I decided to stay on. I wrote to Bruce and broke off our engagement.'

Nadia looked across at us and took a sip of her wine. 'That's such a sad story, Elizabeth,' she said.

'I suppose,' said the Miss Sahib. 'But it was a long time ago and I didn't have much choice. Those were the days when it took two or three months to travel by ship from India to America. You couldn't just hop on a plane. Besides, I felt I was called to go back and take over CMCH. Once I returned to Shakkarganj, I was too busy to get married.'

After an awkward silence, Nadia asked me to carve the turkey and we sat down to eat. Before I served her, I noticed that the Miss Sahib bowed her head briefly in prayer.

A couple of years later, Miss Cranston called me to say that she'd been diagnosed with the early stages of dementia. She told me this in a flat, unemotional tone and I didn't know what to say, trying to console her but also confused about how I felt. I remember thinking that if she lost her memory, a part of me would be erased. The next weekend Nadia and I went to see her. She didn't seem upset and spent most of the time explaining the practical details and arrangements she'd made. Through friends in the church she'd found an assisted living facility near Hartford, where she was going to move, 'before I get too forgetful'.

To me, she seemed fine, though she repeated herself a couple of times and forgot Nadia's name. Miss Cranston didn't want any help from us and said she'd worked everything out for herself. 'I don't want to be a burden on you or anyone else,' she said. 'But I have one request.'

'Of course,' I replied.

'Daniel, I want you to take the steamer trunk,' she said. 'It contains a lot of stuff that you can throw out but maybe some of it will mean something to you.'

With difficulty, Nadia and I were able to drag the trunk out of Miss Cranston's cupboard and down the stairs to my car, which had plenty of space in the back. Later, when we got home and I opened the trunk, a familiar smell of old paper filled my nostrils, immediately taking me back to Shakkarganj and the Miss Sahib's dufter. It was a slightly musty, dry sort of odour, not unpleasant but with a hint of desiccation. Picking up one of the files, I inhaled the aroma and remembered standing by the Miss Sahib's desk, watching her typing or doing accounts.

Aside from the papers, the trunk contained a number of random objects like rubber stamps and an inkpad, which she had used for official documents. I also found a paper punch that I remember playing with as a boy, making holes in scrap paper and then collecting the circular bits of confetti. When Ezekiel Masih emptied Miss Cranston's desk, he must have put everything in the trunk for there were stubs of pencils and well-worn erasers, receipt books, even a spare set of keys for her jeep. There was a box of carbon paper too that looked as if it could still be used. When I rubbed one corner, it left a dark smudge on my fingertips. Along with this were a couple of metal cash boxes containing coins and one-rupee notes, as well as paper clips and safety pins. I even found an empty rifle shell with a dent in the primer and a residual smell of cordite. Blowing across the end of it I could make a low whistle, something the Miss Sahib had taught me.

The other object that I discovered, tucked away inside a shoebox full of odds and ends, was a small ivory elephant that had fascinated me as a child. The Miss Sahib kept it in one of the pigeonholes of her desk and she would let me take it down and hold it in my hands. I used to think it was the most precious thing in the world, not because it was made of ivory but because it was so intricately carved into a lifelike, miniature creature. Miss Cranston once told me that it was a gift from her mother. Discovering the tiny elephant again in the steamer trunk, I felt as if it were a personal heirloom, a totem object linking me to an ancestral past. The ivory had turned a creamy colour with age but the graven image of the elephant remained as perfect as I recalled from the first time I had held it in my hands.

Near the top of the trunk, I also found the unfinished typescript of Miss Cranston's *A New Jungle Book*. She must have added it later, along with a bundle of files about her arrest and deportation, court documents in both Hindi and English, as well as a chart of her fingerprints in smudged blue ink on a crude-looking form. There was also a clear plastic file containing carbon copies of the letters she wrote to me after I went off to college. Most of these, I'd thrown away as soon as I received them, without even reading what she wrote, or else I tore them up in a fit of frustration and bitterness. In her methodical, fastidious manner Miss Cranston had made copies the way she did with all her letters, the sooty grey impressions of the carbon paper smudging the page. I had to wonder whether she'd kept these copies for herself or were they meant for me to discover, years later? Reading them carefully I tried to understand her motives, putting together fragments of the past, to reach some sense of equanimity and absolution.

THREE

Leaving the compound in a hired jeep that Pradeep has organized for me, we set off along the narrow road heading north towards Hathi Talao Wildlife Sanctuary. The driver's name is Jackie. He lives on the compound, a young man in his twenties. Within a few minutes, I can see a procession of bullock carts loaded with sugar cane, heading in the direction of the factory. At the side of the road, in one village we pass, farmers are making raw gur, boiling syrup in an open vat over a mud-plastered hearth fuelled mostly by dry stalks of squeezed sugar cane. Asking Jackie to pull over, I walk across to buy a kilo of gur, which has been formed into fist-sized lumps, a dull orange colour. Breaking off a chunk, I put a piece in my mouth. Though I haven't eaten gur for years, it immediately takes me back to my childhood—a sharp, sweet flavour that makes my teeth and gums itch with pleasure. At this time of year, I remember hawkers who would come by the gate of the compound selling gur for less than a rupee a kilo. Miss Cranston would often buy a basketful and get the cooks to melt the gur and mix it with peanuts to make brittle that we devoured, even before it had cooled and hardened completely.

Another kilometre on ahead, the sulphurous stink of the sugar factory becomes almost unbearable. As a boy, I could never understand how something as sweet and pure as sugar could give off such a nauseating stench. Most of the road is blocked with bullock carts lined up to deliver sugar cane. We have to drive off onto a rutted detour along one side. A signboard above the gate identifies the mill as the Shiv Shakti Sugar Works. I hold my breath, as we drive past but the jeep has to slow down because of the overloaded carts and

I finally exhale, before covering my nose and drawing the sickening odour into my lungs.

Soon, however, we leave the mill behind and are out in the countryside again, where seemingly endless fields of sugar cane are waiting to be harvested. The road is lined on either side with shisham and babool trees that cast puddled shadows on the weathered asphalt. By a ditch at the side of the road, I see two children crouching next to a stagnant pool, watching a white egret poised at the water's edge. Offering Jackie some gur, I break off another piece and slip it into my mouth, closing my eyes as the intense, raw sweetness sears my throat.

Yesterday, we buried Miss Cranston's ashes. Most of the compound community showed up to pay their respects. Some of the women were crying, dabbing their eyes with the ends of their dupattas. Reverend Nazareth said a long prayer in which he praised the missionaries for their sacrifices and called the Miss Sahib, 'a devoted daughter of Christ'. Her ashes were in a brass urn that the funeral home had provided. Always organized and self-reliant, Miss Cranston had made arrangements for her own cremation while she was still alive, paying the funeral home in advance and leaving instructions for them to contact me. After I placed the urn in the hole next to her father's grave, I said a few words of thanks, speaking awkwardly in Hindustani, overcome by emotions I hadn't expected. We then sang a hymn:

> *Abide with me: fast falls the eventide;*
> *the darkness deepens; Lord, with me abide.*
> *When other helpers fail and comforts flee,*
> *Help of the helpless, O abide with me.*

When the last verse trailed away, Reverend Nazareth gestured for me to drop a handful of earth into the grave. I heard it rattle against the urn. The rest of the congregation followed my lead and when everyone had finished, one of the men shovelled the remaining soil into the hole, filling it up.

Three months ago, soon after the Miss Sahib died, I found a

Christmas card from Pradeep among her papers. Writing to him, I asked if he could help with the burial of her ashes. In my letter, I gave my email address and he replied as soon as he got it. Later, after the date for my trip was set, I asked if there was any way that I could visit Hathi Talao National Park. Pradeep said it would be no problem, because he has connections with the forest department. One of his students is the son of the DFO, divisional forest officer. He was able to book a rest house for me and even offered to come along, though I wrote to say that I preferred to visit the sanctuary on my own.

Day before yesterday, when Pradeep gave me my entry permit for the park and the rest of the receipts, he refused to take any money from me at first, but I insisted on repaying him. We were sitting in the dufter, which is now his office where he has a computer. He laughed when he told me that his son had to teach him how to use it. On one of the other desks, where Pradeep's assistant sits, I noticed the Miss Sahib's old typewriter.

Going across, I hesitated then placed my fingers on the keys.

'Do you still use this?' I asked.

Pradeep glanced across and shook his head. 'Only when we need to fill out government forms that aren't available online. The problem is that you can't get typewriter ribbons these days.'

Under the pressure of my fingers, I felt the keys rising, though I released them before they touched the roller. I could still remember the first time I typed my name and how the Miss Sahib taught me to spell 'Mowgli'.

Twelve kilometres out of Shakkarganj, we join the main highway to Pilibhit and Tanakpur, though after another half hour, we turn off the main route and onto a narrower road again. To the east of Pilibhit is a larger tiger reserve. Hathi Talao lies to the north-west in a cluster of low hills and ravines along the Bhabar Naddi, a small river that drains into the Sarda. These forests were once the hunting preserve of the Nawab of Khempur, a minor principality in Rohilkhand.

Soon, I can see the blue outlines of the ridges rising above the cultivated plains. Most of the fields are planted with sugar cane but also arhar dal and mango orchards. Jackie says this area is less prosperous than Shakkarganj.

'Are there still dacoits in this region?' I ask.

'Of course,' he replies with a grin. 'Not as many as before. But these days they mostly smuggle drugs from Nepal.'

'Do they still stop people on the highway at night?' I ask.

He shakes his head. 'Not as much. Dacoits have become very modern now. They all have mobile phones and use Facebook.'

'What about kidnappings?'

'Sometimes....'

I remember this part of the drive from when Miss Cranston would bring us here in her jeep, riding with the other boys in the trailer. We pass the outskirts of Khempur, a dusty, unimpressive town with the domed silhouette of the Nawab's palace and a mosque with four minarets like sharpened pencils. Further on, we enter the buffer zone of the park, a sparse, degraded belt of jungle full of grazing cattle and goats. Most of the lower branches on the trees have been lopped for fodder and firewood. Again, I have a clear memory of driving along this road. For our trips to Hathi Talao, the Miss Sahib would remove the canvas roof of her jeep so that her hair blew about in the wind. One time we had a flat tyre along this stretch of the road. Miss Cranston changed the wheel herself while the rest of us watched as she loosened the lug nuts and cranked the handle to raise the jack. With a reassuring smile, she told us that if we had another flat tyre we'd be 'stuck here forever'. I was terrified that a tiger might arrive and eat us.

The main gate of the sanctuary is an ugly concrete archway painted green with red lettering: Hathi Talao Tiger Reserve. Next to this is a sign listing rules and regulations. A surly forest ranger inspects my permit. Pradeep has given his address as mine. He has also instructed me to speak only in Hindi and not to admit that I am a foreigner because the rates are much higher for visitors from abroad. The ranger asks me a few questions and then scribbles his signature on the permit. Though we have already been charged for the jeep and driver, he insists that we must pay those fees again. Jackie begins to argue but I stop him and hand over a thousand rupees, for which we receive no receipt.

'These are the real dacoits,' says Jackie as we climb back into his vehicle. 'All they care about is filling their own pockets.'

My booking is for two nights at Jhumri Rest House, another twelve kilometres inside the park. According to the regulations, one of the forest guards must accompany us as a guide and we wait until he is called. Fortunately, the guard turns out to be a pleasant, cheerful young man named Riaz Ahmed with a timid smile and a camouflage coat. As we enter the park, he asks me where I am from and I tell him Shakkarganj.

'Why are you coming here to Hathi Talao?' he says, giving me a sceptical look. 'If you want to see a tiger, there's a much better chance in Corbett Park or even Pilibhit. We only have five tigers in this forest.'

'It doesn't matter if I don't see a tiger,' I reassure him. 'I came here many years ago, when I was a boy. My main reason for visiting is to see the jungle again.'

He nods and takes a packet of chewing tobacco out of his shirt pocket. Opening it, he crushes and mixes it in the palm of his hand before tucking the tobacco inside his lower lip. After that, he remains silent for most of the ride.

As we drive through the forest, we see a couple of peacocks that race across the dirt road and into the bushes. Further on, a herd of chital is grazing in a clearing. Jackie slows the jeep and the deer raise their heads in alarm, dashing out of sight, as if we have fired a gun at them.

'Is there much poaching still?'

Riaz nods, then spits out his window.

'There's always poaching,' he says in a cynical tone. 'If you catch one gang, another starts up. It's a constant battle.'

'Are there wild elephants?' I ask.

'Yes, three separate herds, almost forty altogether, but only two big tuskers,' he replies, then looks at me curiously. 'Are you from Madras?'

'No,' I say. 'Why?'

'Because your Hindi isn't very good.' He says this without meaning to be rude, then falls silent again as the tobacco juice fills his mouth.

Watching the columns of trees pass by and the green blur of foliage, I wonder whether my visit to the park will be a waste of time. What am I really hoping to find? Though I've said I'm not interested in spotting a tiger, part of me is on the lookout for a flash of black stripes and saffron fur within the verdant shadows of the jungle. But more than that, my eyes search the layered canopy of trees and tangled undergrowth for anything that might look familiar. It isn't that I expect to recover secrets from my feral past, certainly not the truth behind my rescue or any direct inheritance from Kipling's myth of Mowgli's youth. Maybe it is something much older and more obscure that I'm pursuing. Perhaps, consciously or unconsciously, I want to discover an evolutionary memory, recognizing a shadow of ancestral dreams, a momentary flicker of consciousness connecting me to distant origins.

As we drive along, crossing a dry riverbed, where the forest road turns to sand, with round rocks and boulders lying about like scattered pieces of a mosaic, I scan the edges of the forest as if searching for primal figures, hunter-gatherers who once stalked game along this seasonal watercourse, two or three millennia ago. Though riding in a vehicle with a driver and a guard, I feel as if I am alone, connected to another part of myself that crouches on the periphery of my vision, attentive to the movement of the air and leaves, stems of bamboo twitching in the breeze, a muffled bird call puncturing the primordial silence.

After a while, we come upon a troop of langur monkeys feeding in a grove of amla trees. Riaz identifies the sour fruit and when Jackie stops the jeep beneath one of the trees, the langurs look down at us as if they are trying to recognize who we are. They seem nervous in our presence but do not shy away, gnawing at the pale green fruit. In the bushes below, Riaz points out the half-hidden shape of a sambar, feeding on amla that the monkeys have dropped on the ground.

Driving on, we cross a bridge over a stream, where another road comes in from the hills. 'Where does that go?' I ask.

'Into the core zone of the park,' Riaz replies. 'Visitors aren't allowed.'

After he says this, I feel an immediate urge to take that route, as if somehow the core of the sanctuary contains the secret I am looking for.

'Have you been there?' I ask.

'Many times,' he replies, 'when we go on patrol.'

'Are there more animals in that section of the forest?'

'Some,' he says, waving one hand in a noncommittal gesture, 'but the jungle is very thick and you cannot see them easily.'

As we turn a hairpin bend, climbing out of the streambed beyond the bridge, Jackie suddenly brakes at the top of the embankment.

'Hathi,' he says in a whisper.

At first, I cannot see them and strain my eyes, peering through the dusty windscreen at the road ahead, which winds its way between a corridor of trees. Then, all at once, an elephant materializes amidst the leaves, its massive, grey shape moving out of the shadows into a shaft of light that penetrates the leaves overhead.

'Where is your camera?' Riaz mutters.

Foolishly, I have left it packed in my luggage at the back. The elephant, a large female, watches us with a dubious expression, as if gauging whether we pose a threat or not. Swaying gracefully, she stands her ground but I sense nothing dangerous in her demeanour. We are safe inside the jeep and the elephants are seventy-five metres away, at least. Three others have now emerged from the margins of the jungle, a younger male with sharp, slender tusks and two adult females. Several others are feeding just out of sight and I hear a branch break and leaves rustling to our right. Eventually, over the next ten minutes, the elephants amble onto the road and eye us from a distance. None of them seem to be in a hurry, and we wait until they have crossed over, eleven of them altogether, in a disorderly procession. Watching their lumbering movements, I imagine myself riding atop the matriarch as she leads the others away and out of sight.

When Riaz gives Jackie a signal, he starts the jeep again and we drive slowly forward. In the dust at the side of the road, I can see huge, flat prints and clods of dung but there is no other sign of the elephants. It is remarkable that creatures as huge as these can vanish so quickly.

After another five minutes, we arrive at Jhumri Rest House, turning off the main forest road and passing through a gate that Riaz opens. A barbed wire fence encloses the rest house complex, which includes the main bungalow and a line of quarters for the caretaker and guards. As we pull up, an elderly man in wrinkled khaki appears. He salutes and greets me, 'Salaam Sahib!' The chowkidar looks as if he might be eighty, though Mor Singh later tells me that he is sixty-five, my age.

Years ago, I stayed here with Miss Cranston, when she brought a group of us for a weeklong outing in the sanctuary. The rest house has been painted with a recent coat of whitewash but otherwise it seems the same. Going across to the edge of the lawn, where it slopes down into the forest, I can see the shallow river below, flowing along a rocky channel fringed with trees.

Bimla has packed a cardboard box of provisions and vegetables, which Mor Singh takes charge of, assuring us that he will cook our meals. One of the two suites in the rest house is mine, with a dining room, off which is a bedroom, and a bath. There are no other visitors tonight though Mor Singh says another group is expected day after tomorrow. Most of the chairs are broken and the dining table is stained and cracked. My bed is a sagging string charpoy with a thin foam mattress covered in frayed pink fabric. Fortunately, Bimla has sent sheets and a quilt for my bedding. The bathroom has a squat latrine with a tap protruding from the wall, as well as an old wooden washstand and a dented aluminium basin. A mirror hangs from a nail and a red plastic bucket sits upside down near the drain. There is no electricity and only a couple of candle stubs stuck to the windowsills.

Though Mor Singh's housekeeping is rudimentary, he is a good cook. By nightfall, we have a meal of vegetables, dal, and rice. Jackie and Riaz are staying in the quarters but I insist they eat with me before it gets completely dark. As we dine on the verandah, I can hear peacocks calling from the edge of the forest and the sharp alarm cries of chital.

'Probably a leopard nearby,' says Riaz.

It is cooler in the forest than it was in Shakkarganj. Following dinner, I ask if we can light a fire because it is too early to go to bed. There is plenty of dead wood and Riaz soon has a blaze going. On the signboard at the main gate there was a notice that fires are not permitted. When I mention this, Riaz shrugs and says that during this season, early spring, the forest isn't dry enough for there to be a risk of wildfires. Jackie brings a chair for me and the others sit cross-legged on the grass, gazing into the flames. I retrieve a bottle of Scotch from my luggage, a single malt with an unpronounceable name that was on sale at Duty Free. Earlier, in Shakkarganj, I offered Pradeep a drink but he declined, saying he gave up alcohol ten years ago after suffering a bad case of hepatitis.

When I ask the others if they will join me for a drink, Riaz refuses, as I assumed he would. Jackie also shakes his head, though Mor Singh seems delighted with the idea. Finishing his meal hurriedly after we have eaten, he fetches a couple of glass tumblers from his kitchen, both of which are chipped along the rim.

'This whisky is from Scotland,' I say. 'It's twelve years old.'

'How much did it cost, Sahib?' Mor Singh asks, as I peel open the cap and uncork the bottle.

Doing a rough calculation in my head, I reply, 'Five thousand rupees.'

The old chowkidar laughs and Riaz shakes his head in amazement.

'It must be very strong,' he says.

'No,' I explain. 'The alcohol content is the same but people savour this whisky for its flavour.' My Hindi betrays me and I have to use twice as many words as necessary to get the meaning across.

'You could buy a dozen bottles of rum for that price,' says Mor Singh, laughing as I pour an inch of the amber liquid into his glass.

'Since when do you drink rum, Uncle?' Jackie teases him. 'Out here in the jungle, you'd be lucky to get even country liquor.'

The chowkidar sniffs at the whisky cautiously as I pour myself a drink and raise my glass. 'Cheers!'

Mor Singh lifts his tumbler ceremoniously as Riaz and Jackie watch us with amusement, the firelight reflecting off their faces. Taking a sip of whisky, I find it has a peaty taste, harsher than I like, but drinkable. Meanwhile, the chowkidar swallows his drink in a single gulp. For a moment, he looks stunned, then his shoulders shudder and I can see tears forming in his eyes, not from emotion, but from the jolt of Scotch. The other two are laughing now as they watch Mor Singh, who is speechless for almost a minute.

When he recovers, he looks at me with an accusing expression. 'What have you given me to drink, Sahib? It tastes like kerosene!' he complains. 'I can buy that for twenty-two rupees a litre!'

By now Jackie and Riaz are in hysterics, their laughter as combustible as the dry branches we stack on the flames. Leaning back in my chair, I feel the whisky unknotting my nerves and laugh along with the others. We are strangers but the darkness of the forest and the circle of firelight creates an aura of companionship. After a few minutes, Mor Singh allows himself to be persuaded to have another drink, though he adds an equal measure of water this time.

'There used to be a ruined temple in the forest,' I say, once the hilarity subsides. 'Is it still there?'

Riaz nods his head. 'Yes, but nobody goes there any more.'

'I'd like to see it if I can.'

'The road is very bad...' he says. 'With a 4X4 vehicle it is possible but why would you want to see it? There's hardly anything left and the jungle has grown over most of the ruins.'

'I remember it clearly and I'd like to get a photograph,' I answer, not wanting to explain too much. 'Is the temple very old?'

Mor Singh takes a sip of his drink and grimaces.

'Certainly more than a hundred years, perhaps a hundred and fifty,' he says. 'The Nawab of Khempur built it when the British were still in power.'

'That's true,' Riaz agrees. 'I've heard this story as well.'

'But why would a Muslim ruler build a Hindu temple in the middle of the jungle?' I ask.

Mor Singh fumbles in his pocket and takes out a packet of bidis, lighting one with a smouldering twig from the fire. Exhaling a cloud of smoke, he begins the story.

> The Nawab was a great shikari and these forests were his private hunting grounds. Nobody was allowed to enter the jungle in those days without his permission. He shot many tigers here and used to bring his trained elephants, along with dozens of guests, Englishmen and others. It was always a huge operation and they would set up camp in the forest. Though he ruled over a small territory and had less wealth than other princely states like Rampur, the Nawab was a proud Rohilla Pathan, a descendant of Afghan warriors who once fought alongside the Mughals. His family had been given Khempur as their jagir during the time of Aurangzeb. Unfortunately for the Nawab, he had no children, though he married three wives. It was one of his greatest disappointments and he consulted many hakims and European doctors but without success.

Warming to the tale, Mor Singh clears his throat and his voice takes on the tone of a rustic raconteur, with a timeless note of omniscience.

> One day, he was hunting in this forest, riding atop his favourite elephant when he came to a hidden clearing, where a year-round spring flowed out of the rocks, forming a pool encircled by trees. Sitting in the shade of one of the trees was a sadhu, an aged mendicant, with long, matted hair, his body dusted with ash. Nearby, the sadhu had built a hut of bamboo and thatch. The Nawab was furious—he was known for his short temper—and ordered his men to arrest the sadhu and expel him from the forest. The mendicant seemed unperturbed but he told the Nawab's officers that as long as they held him captive, none of the animals in the jungle could be killed. They ignored his warnings and sent him away with two guards who were told to escort him to Khempur and from there to Haridwar.

The next day a tiger appeared in front of the hunting party. Nawab Sahib fired but his bullet went wide, though the tiger was standing broadside, well within range. After the elephants pursued the tiger, it appeared once more. Again, the Nawab fired and missed. When this happened a third time, he threw his rifle away in disgust. One of his officers approached and asked permission to speak, explaining what the sadhu had said.

Still enraged, the Nawab abused his officer but when they got back to camp, he had a change of mind and gave orders that the sadhu be brought before him. Eventually, the mendicant returned with his escort and he was delivered into the presence of the Nawab, who angrily asked how he dared trespass in the forest. The sadhu simply said that he had taken sanyaas, renouncing his worldly possessions and retreating into the jungle, living amongst wild animals and feeding on whatever fruit and nuts he could gather. The Nawab asked why he wasn't afraid of cobras, tigers and elephants, being unarmed in the jungle.

'They are not my enemies,' the sadhu replied. 'The animals protect me. This forest is the realm of Lord Shiva who sits in meditation beneath the cobra's hood while the tiger is a companion of the goddess and the elephants are Lord Ganesh.'

Mocking the sadhu for his idolatry and ignorance, the Nawab began to dismiss him. The old mendicant folded his hands and said that he did not wish to be disrespectful, 'but I have heard that Huzoor is childless, your wives without issue.' The proud Rohilla immediately rose to his feet enraged. His officers were terrified that he would cut off the sadhu's head with his sword. But the mendicant seemed unafraid and continued speaking, 'Huzoor will surely be blessed with a son,' he said. 'I can promise that. Your lineage will continue.'

Mor Singh's voice is almost a whisper, barely louder than the crackle of flames in the fire. The three of us have fallen silent and I can see both Riaz and Jackie are listening to every word. It is obvious that the old chowkidar has recounted this story many times before though in the firelight, with the darkness all around us, it seems as if it could be the first time the tale is being told.

> The Nawab's anger subsided slowly and he demanded that the sadhu swear an oath that his prophecy would come true. 'Huzoor, if you let me remain here in the jungle then you will be granted an heir,' said the sadhu, 'but there are only two things I require.' The tall Rohilla glared down at the stooped old man with disdain but the sadhu's voice was clear. 'All I ask is that you give me one pearl from your turban,' said the old man, 'and twelve months from now, when you finally hold your child in your arms, remember to build a temple on this spot.'

Mor Singh pauses as I uncork the bottle and pour him another drink, while he lights a bidi and draws the acrid smoke into his lungs. My glass is also empty but I set it aside, at the foot of my chair. From somewhere behind us I can hear the chuckling sound of a nightjar. Riaz adds another dead branch to the fire and a flurry of bright cinders rise with the smoke.

> The Nawab's hunting turban was made of green silk with a line of pearls stitched along the edge of the uppermost fold. After a moment's hesitation, he reached up and plucked one of the pearls with his fingers, handing it to the old man, who extended his right palm to receive it. Nothing more was said as the sadhu took a step backwards and the Nawab retreated to his tent.
>
> For another week, the hunt continued. Nawab Sahib successfully shot a tiger as well as plenty of other game, though he was subdued by his encounter with the hermit and instructed his shikaris to move camp to another part of the forest. After returning to Khempur, he was reunited with his wives and continued to direct the affairs of state, though people noticed that he had changed. Word of the sadhu's prophecy spread quickly though the Nawab himself said nothing about it. He seemed distracted and absorbed in thought, with little patience for ceremonies and rituals, though he visited the tomb of a Sufi saint on the outskirts of Khempur and offered prayers in private.
>
> Time passed and his subjects waited expectantly for word that

one of the begums might be pregnant but nothing happened. Within the palace there was eager anticipation. As each month went by, the Nawab became more impatient with those around him, losing his temper over minor matters.

Mor Singh flicks the burnt end of his bidi into the fire, then drains the last of his drink. Instead of looking at us, he stares into the flames, as if to spark his memory of the tale.

> After a full year had passed and no child had been conceived, the Nawab gave orders that his elephants be made ready for shikar and set off into the forest. Back then, there were no pucca roads and it took five days for the hunting party to reach the sadhu's hut. By the time they got there the Nawab was in a silent rage, speaking to no one but cursing the sadhu with every breath. His officers and attendants were sure he would kill the hermit for having uttered a false prophecy.
>
> Finally, when the hidden spring came in view, the Nawab gestured for his rifle, though there was no animal in sight. His elephant kneeled and the Rohilla dismounted, waving his retainers aside as he circled the pool on foot. Even from a distance, they could see that the sadhu's hut had collapsed and it was overgrown with weeds. The place seemed deserted but when the Nawab pushed his way through the undergrowth and reached the spot, he noticed a cobra glide out of sight, vanishing into the rocks near the spring. Expecting to find the sadhu's corpse, or evidence of a tiger's kill, the Nawab stepped forward and brushed aside the collapsed remains of the hut. Amidst the wreckage lay a bundle of straw. Leaning down, the Rohilla saw before him a helpless infant less than a few months old, swaddled in leaves. It was a boy—healthy and well-fed. The naked child was awake but silent, content and unafraid.
>
> As the Nawab's party gathered around in amazement, their ruler's anger subsided. Handing his rifle to a gun bearer, he kneeled in the grass and picked the child up in his arms. The baby stared back at him with innocent, impassive eyes as the Nawab

studied the perfect features of the infant's face. The child's fists were clenched but after a moment, the tiny fingers on the boy's right hand opened, revealing a glistening white pearl in his palm.

FOUR

The next morning, we rise early, as the sky begins to brighten beyond a dark colonnade of trees. Mor Singh has brewed us each a strong, sweet glass of tea that I drink on the verandah of the rest house, barely able to make out a pale fleece of mist hovering over the wet grass. The ashes of our campfire have been doused by dew.

With some difficulty, Jackie gets his jeep started but once the diesel engine ignites it settles into a steady, percussive rumble. I put on an extra layer and take my seat in front, my camera in my lap, while Riaz scrambles into the back.

'Today, we'll see a tiger,' he assures me.

'What about the temple?' I ask.

He hesitates, then nods. 'It's off the main road, but if you are interested, we can go there later, once we've done a circuit of the park.' We speak in whispers, our breath condensing in the cold half-light of dawn. Last evening, I went to bed around ten o'clock, after Mor Singh fell silent and we finally let the fire die down. Once I'd blown out the candle and crawled under my quilt, the darkness was complete, as if I were entombed in a cave. Though I felt exhausted, my mind kept racing, without any logical progression of thoughts, as if a rabble of memories and voices were clashing in my mind—things Miss Cranston said to me when I was a boy, recent conversations with Pradeep, Mor Singh's story of the Nawab and a random image of a woman I saw on the plane, her hair the colour of iodine.

The jeep nudges forward as Jackie wrestles with the gears but soon we are on our way. I feel a sense of excitement and anticipation, as if we are about to enter an unexplored landscape. Just outside the gate, a sounder of wild boar race across the road in front of us, eight or ten of them like scruffy miscreants escaping from the scene of a crime.

Further on, we see fresh evidence of elephants, steaming clods of dung and broken branches.

'This is a different herd,' says Riaz. 'Not those we saw yesterday. These elephants have several young calves, only a few months old.'

With the sound of the jeep there is very little else that I can hear but when we come to a crossing, where another forest track joins the main road, Riaz signals for Jackie to stop and switch off the engine.

The silence is like a vacuum that gradually fills with sounds, the whistle of an unknown bird and then the chatter of jungle babblers. A barking deer, off in the distance, gives a tentative alarm call, like the startled yelp of a dog. My eyes survey the grey-green shadows of the forest, searching for movement. Jackie coughs into his fist. Then we hear another alarm call, this one louder, a deeper, metallic sound. Riaz raises his hand and we hold our breath. The alarm is repeated. I can tell it is coming from the side road, off to our left.

'Sambar,' Riaz whispers. 'There's a tiger nearby.'

He signals to Jackie, who starts the vehicle and reverses, then turns off onto the side road, towards the alarm. We drive slowly as the forest opens out into a patch of high grass. A tawny owl takes flight from a branch overhead.

We stop once more and the engine dies abruptly as Jackie switches it off. Almost immediately, the sambar's call is repeated, no more than forty metres away, a sharp, insistent cry.

Riaz grins at me and points into the grass. We wait.

A junglefowl gives a shrill, cackling call, similar to the roosters crowing on the compound but with a note of panic. Though everything is still, the sounds seem to trace invisible movements in the grass, the sambar calling once again and another answering from the right. Riaz leans forward intently, trying to read the signals. I feel a prickling sense of anticipation between my shoulder blades.

For half an hour, we continue to wait but gradually the alarm cries subside, replaced by a chaotic medley of bird calls. A drongo chases an insect overhead, a woodpecker shrieks and then begins to rattle a dead tree, as if typing a message with its beak. There are other sounds too, a murmur of flies and invisible creatures crawling about in the litter of leaves. By the time Riaz shakes his head in disappointment, the sun has begun to filter through the leaves.

'The tiger has gone,' says Riaz, directing Jackie to drive on ahead while explaining, '...this road will take us to the temple.' But almost as soon as we start moving, he taps Jackie on the shoulder.

'Look there,' he says to me, pointing at the ground beside us.

Other than dust and grass at the side of the road, I can see nothing.

'There,' Riaz insists. 'A pugmark.'

Staring down, I finally spot the tiger's print, faint but unmistakable, the outline of the predator's paw, with its broad pad and round toes.

'We missed seeing her by a few minutes,' Riaz whispers. 'She must have crossed over just ahead of us, a big tigress who hunts in this area. Maybe she is headed in the direction of the temple.'

Jackie lets out the clutch and we lurch forward, continuing along the side road for ten minutes, until an overgrown track comes in from the right. Riaz gestures for Jackie to turn off and we enter heavy cover, branches and leaves brushing against both sides of the jeep. After some distance, the track pitches down sharply into a ravine and we descend, until our route is blocked by a fallen tree. Unconcerned about the possible presence of a tiger, Riaz hops down from the jeep and drags the upper branches to one side, as Jackie manoeuvres around the tree. I wonder if I should suggest we turn back but Riaz seems confident that we will reach the temple. Crossing a streambed full of rocks, Jackie has to shift into four-wheel drive as we blunder across and up a sand bank. I can see no animals though the forest is so thick, they could be anywhere behind the dense curtain of leaves. Finally, after another ten minutes of rough driving, we come to a clearing where Riaz tells Jackie to stop. Sunlight is streaming through gaps in the trees and reflecting off a pool of water, thirty metres across, surrounded by reeds. At the edge of the pond I spot a broken wall and a stone pillar wreathed in creepers.

Glancing at Riaz, I ask, 'Is it safe to get out of the jeep?'

He makes a casual, complacent gesture with one hand and nods.

'No problem,' he says in English.

Climbing down from the jeep I take my camera out of its case and focus on the ruins, snapping a couple of pictures before moving closer. From this angle I can see more of the abandoned temple, including a stone wall and what looks like part of a dome that has caved in. A wild fig tree grows up one side of the shrine, its sinuous roots clutching at cracks between the rocks. I am nervous about moving too far away from the jeep but Riaz leads me through the waist-high grass. We scramble over a broken parapet and across a marshy ditch then crawl up a pile of stones where another wall has collapsed. Riaz holds out his hand and helps me up onto the plinth of the temple.

Remembering how Miss Cranston and I observed this scene so many years ago, with a peacock perched on one of the ruined walls at sunset, I hear her words again: 'Praying to an elephant isn't the worst thing someone can do. Surely, it's no cause for damnation.' I also recall the scenes from the story she wrote, her retelling of *The Jungle Book*, in which she describes this place and the boy burying a pair of blood-stained tusks beneath the ruins.

'Do you know when this temple was abandoned?' I ask Riaz.

He shakes his head. 'Long ago.'

'Is it a Ganesh temple?'

'That's what they say, but the idols have all been removed.' Riaz points towards the vacant interior of the shrine.

'I read somewhere that elephants come here to worship,' I say.

He laughs. 'Elephants drink at this pond but they don't pray to any gods, not even Ganesh.'

A turquoise kingfisher hovers over the reeds at the water's edge.

'Do you think the story Mor Singh told us last night is true?' I ask.

Riaz pauses for a moment, looking around him at the remains of the temple. 'It's a story,' he says. 'It could be true. It could be false.'

'But you've heard that the Nawab of Khempur built this temple. Isn't that a fact?' I persist.

'Yes, there is no doubt, it was built by the Nawab...but the sadhu...and the child with the pearl in his hand...' Riaz shrugs and laughs, 'It is a legend or a myth. Who knows?'

'Do you think a child could survive alone in this jungle, even for a day?'

'No,' he says, shaking his head decisively. 'There are too many predators.'

'But in a story?'

'Yes, of course. In a story anything is possible,' says Riaz.

'Could a human being be raised by wild animals, monkeys and elephants, for example?' I ask.

Riaz shakes his head. 'I've heard of these things but it is just folklore and imagination. How could it be true?'

'This mandir, this temple, was built to contain and preserve ancient stories,' I say. 'It's a sanctuary, just like a church...or a masjid.'

Riaz makes a non-committal gesture with one hand and looks away.

'The whole forest is a sanctuary,' he says, reaching into his pocket and taking out a pouch of chewing tobacco, as if to signal that he doesn't want to carry on with this conversation.

Entering what remains of the temple, I am no longer worried that a tigress might appear. A small lizard, four inches long, crawls over one of the stones and ducks out of sight. The rocks have been carefully cut and fitted together but over time the roots and moisture have loosened their foundations, the marshy ground subsiding. Perhaps an earthquake toppled these walls. There is some decoration, a floral design as well as geometric patterns that have all but worn away. It smells of bats and a musky odour that could be the scent of a civet or some kind of jungle cat.

Turning back towards the pond, I descend the steps where a stone channel directs the flow of the spring as it emerges from beneath the ruined shrine. A clear vein of water seeps out as a trickle, with a film of green scum on either side, then spatters onto a flat rock at the edge of the pool. After taking a few more photographs, I set my camera aside.

From the inside pocket of my jacket, I remove a small parcel. It feels lighter than I remember, as I peel away the layers of plastic and tissue paper in which it is wrapped, stuffing them back into my pocket. The tiny, ivory elephant lies within the cupped palm of my hand. Yellowed with age it still has a creamy lustre and a hard, smooth texture.

Though the elephant is smaller than the length of my thumb, about the size of a chess piece, it is intricately carved, the shape of its ears and tiny eyes looking out at me with a benevolent gaze. Each toenail has been delicately fashioned, as well as the tail and wrinkles on its skin. The trunk curls up to one side, as if the miniature animal were about to spray water on itself. Though fashioned from a tusk, this tiny elephant has none of its own.

Years ago, when I first took it down from one of the pigeonholes in Miss Cranston's desk and asked her why it had no tusks, she answered me in her patient, gentle voice.

'It's a female, Mowgli,' the Miss Sahib said, smiling and winking at me. 'Only males are tuskers, though matriarchs rule the herd.'

Part of me wants to cradle the elephant in my hand forever and not let go but I have already made up my mind. The water at the foot of the stone steps is a murky jade colour, with strands of algae floating on top. I cannot see the bottom as I release the ivory elephant from my grasp. Falling, it makes a splash. Beneath spreading rings of water, the pale, white shape disappears into the green depths of the forest pool.

IV
ELEPHANT CHILD

As the mother elephant wades into the pond, brushing aside the reeds with her trunk, the boy feels the cool water reach his toes. Seated on the matriarch's back, he can see the ruined steps where a spring flows out of the rocks. The rest of the herd has moved off into the jungle and the two of them are alone, surrounded by the silence of the trees. The boy has often plunged into this pool, swimming here by himself. The only sound is the rustling of reeds and the water's hushed whisper, as it parts around the elephant's shoulders. She swims to the centre of the pond with graceful buoyancy that belies her bulk, as much a creature of the water as she is of the land.

The boy remains on her back until the elephant submerges herself completely, disappearing beneath the surface and descending into the watery womb of the forest pool. He slides away from her and sweeps both arms wide, in a single stroke, before diving under himself, his body arching like a bow. The water is clearer at the centre of the pool than it was near the shore. When he opens his eyes, the boy can see the elephant beneath him, her ears waving and her trunk swaying from side to side, two streams of bubbles trickling from her nostrils. She moves through the water with an ease that makes her seem as weightless as a shadow. Her feet touch the bottom lightly, like a dancer. Exhaling a cloud of bubbles, the boy reaches out with both arms, kicking his legs in a strong, steady rhythm until the tips of his fingers finally brush against the elephant's rough hide, after which he turns and ascends towards the opaque dome of light above them.

The boy has nothing to fear as the water holds him in its fluid embrace. Moments later, he breaks the surface and gasps for air. Treading water, he waits for the matriarch to appear but after a minute has passed, he wonders if she will ever rise out of the pool again, or disappear forever. He thinks of diving down once more but then he sees ripples crease the surface and the elephant's trunk emerges like a serpent uncoiling out of the pool and spraying a jet of water into the air. Slowly, the rest of her head appears and her small, gem-like eyes blink at him with a knowing look.

He can hear the last flutter of breath exhaled and then the swelling *sound of her huge lungs filling with air. The boy and the elephant do not speak but as he swims around her, gliding over the contours of her back, he can hear the deep resonance of a song. Slipping underwater again, he listens to the vibrations that surround him and moves to the rhythm of her voice. It seems as if the pool itself is filled with sound, reverberating from the hollow chambers of the elephant's chest. As the boy dives beneath her, the pressure on his ears amplifies the song, which encircles him like invisible waves of music agitating the still water.*

The song has a strange sadness to it, full of plaintive harmonies, as well as a wild, mysterious tempo that seems to echo the drumming of his heart. The boy swims in circles around the elephant as she floats just below the surface of the pool, her legs moving slowly like the roots of a tree released from the soil.

Again, he rises to the surface, as if lifted by the song,
Swimming into the green sunlight,
Reborn